"Oh my gosh! Kailen! It is true! Your wings are beautiful!" They were beautiful; they were like the wings of an exotic butterfly. They shimmered in bold shades of green and blue. I looked around and I noticed several more pairs of elaborately decorated wings. My mouth hung open in amazement.

"Callie, look at your wings." Kailen said in awe. I turned so that I could look toward my back. My wings were glorious. They were a shimmering gold with elaborate designs scrolled in a darker shade from the top to the bottom. I could hardly believe that they were real.

Stay

A Callie Rose Novel

C.C. Jackson

Edited By Shannon Hicks

Copyright 2011 C.C. Jackson

4

This book is dedicated to my wonderful husband and my three awesome sons. Without your humor and patience this project would never have been possible.

Stay

1

Lying in my room in the dark, I fought hard to get a grasp on what it was that had suddenly ripped me from my sleep. I was completely disoriented and worse, I was still trembling from the nightmare that I had just been having. It just felt so real.

In my dream, I was running down a dark road fleeing from a city that was engulfed in flames. I tripped and stumbled along the way, scraping my knee and palms. I vividly remember the pain that ripped through my hands as I fought to keep my balance and to keep running.

The smoke was filled with a strong bitter odor that scorched my throat and eyes. It was like a combination of burning rubber and chemicals. I struggled with each breath. I was nearly choking.

I repeatedly looked back over my shoulder as I ran, trying to get a glimpse of whatever it was that I was so convinced was chasing me. My lungs burned and my muscles were screaming in pain, but the terror that I felt compelled me to keep moving.

I turned again to see how close my pursuer was getting, only this time I completely lost my balance and fell hard onto the asphalt, scraping my shoulder and forehead as I slid to a stop.

Tears began to stream down my face and tremors ripped through my body as I came to the realization that I would not escape.

Frantically, I searched the darkness and shadows. I caught a movement out of the corner of my eye. Before I knew what was happening, he was on me and I was screaming.

I woke up to find that I was still in my bed. The sheets and blanket were a twisted mess and I struggled to free my legs from them. I could still feel my tears hot on my face, and I had to work hard to steady my breathing.

I heard it again. I jerked my head up. It was the same sound that woke me from my dream. A loud thud, that seemed to have come from the other side of the room. I froze as I tried to force my eyes to focus in the darkness. I searched the contours of my room with wide eyes. I did not move a muscle and I held my breath.

Nothing looked out of place from what I could tell in the dimly lit room. The only light was what little moonlight made it in through my heavy curtains. I waited and held my breath but nothing else happened. After a few minutes, I finally felt my muscles begin to relax. I let out a long ragged breath, and shook my head in frustration.

"It was only a dream." I said out loud to myself, and I began to settle back into the comforts of my bed.

I was about to close my eyes, hoping not to have any more nightmares, when something happened. It is kind of hard to explain, but the darkness just sort of shifted. There was no light really, just that the darkness seamed to grow darker in the far corner of the room.

I stopped breathing and again, I strained to see in the murky blackness. What was wrong with me? This dream has made me so paranoid.

That is when I heard him. Footsteps came across my floor and in a hurry. I barely had time to sit up. The next thing that I knew, I was being dragged from my bed by my arm and just as I was about to start to screaming for my parents a cold hand clamped down hard across my mouth.

I could not see anything in the blinding darkness, but I could tell that this guy was tall. He was at least half a foot or more taller than I was, and obviously very strong because he propelled me across my room with ease. I clawed and scraped at his arms in an attempt to free myself, but his grip never loosened. He kept one hand wrapped tightly around my waist and the other continued to stifle my scream as he raced toward my open window. I had not even noticed that it was open a few minutes ago. He climbed out, still clutching me to him and carried me out into the cool spring night.

I felt as if I were soaring through the air as he leapt from my second story bedroom window and landed on the ground in a graceful thud. He immediately started running towards the woods behind my house. It did not take long until I found that we were under the cover of the trees. I could smell the sweet scent of the Magnolia trees that my mother was so fond of, and the soft needles of the pine trees tugged at my skin as we sped by them.

My mind started racing. I could not imagine how we were even able to survive a fall like that, let alone for him to be running through the woods with me in his arms. More important, who was this and what did he want with me?

I tried to fight harder. I kicked and clawed at him, but he never slowed. I tried to bite the hand that was covering most of the lower part of my face, but his grip was too tight and I could barely move my jaw. I was struggling just to breathe.

No matter how hard I fought against him he just kept running. I could feel the wind blowing my hair around my face as we moved. I had to shut my eyes to keep them from burning from the cold air.

We darted through the trees in a way that left me baffled. I could not understand how he could move so quickly through them and not run into a branch or trip over a log.

I tried to remember if I had done anything in the last few days that would have angered somebody enough to do something like this to me.

I lived in a small town in southern Louisiana. Nothing ever really happens there.

I went to school, and while I was not really the most popular girl, I did not think that anyone hated me. I have never had a boyfriend, and I just had a few girls that I talked to in school. For the most part, I kept to myself.

After school, I came straight home. I did what little homework that I needed to do and then I hung out on our front porch swing reading the latest vampire novel and listening to 30 Seconds to Mars on my iPod.

My parents came home and did their nightly ritual of cooking, bathing, and TV watching. I did not remember seeing any strange people hanging around like you always hear about on the news.

Believe me, I would have noticed. I lived in a pretty rural area of the south, my nearest neighbor is over a half a mile away. Our yard is pretty much surrounded by woods and swamp. The only thing that should be out there is deer and an occasional raccoon.

What if this was some sadistic serial killer? What in the hell was I going to do? I could not fight him. I could barely breathe, let alone scream. I just needed to try to calm down. I needed to be able to think. He would have to stop eventually. When he did, I would have to be ready to do everything that I could to escape before he hurt me.

He carried me for what felt like an eternity, but he never loosened his grip on my mouth or my waist. All that I can remember seeing are trees. The moon was shining brightly overhead, and occasionally I noticed an opossum or some other animal skitter away from us.

He kept me with my back pressed firmly against his chest. His arm snaked out from under my left armpit and curled across me along my chest.

I could feel the rigid contours of his pecs and his abs through my flimsy t-shirt. He definitely worked out, a lot. He never seemed to tire, or even so much as breathed heavily.

He finally slowed and I was completely lost. I had no idea how far he had carried me, nothing looked familiar. The trees were taller and thicker, nothing like the grand moss covered Live Oak trees that surrounded my home in Louisiana. There were no palmettos, and the terrain was no longer flat and marshy. I thought that I could see tree covered mountains off in the distance.

He carried me through a patch of thick brush using his shoulder and legs to push back the branches and vines that blocked our path. I felt cobwebs string across my face and I wanted to shudder because I was not able to wipe them off me. I was definitely going to end up with poison ivy or worse.

The brush began to thin and eventually we emerged into in a small clearing. I could hear water flowing in a stream somewhere close by.

We headed in the direction of the water and followed it downstream. It curved lazily through the woods and brought us close to an opening in the side of a rocky cliff.

I am not sure what time of the night that I was taken, but the sun was starting to come up over the top of the mountains. I knew that we must have traveled for hours.

Standing in front of the entrance to a cave in the side of the cliff, my captor finally set me down on my feet. My muscles screamed in a sigh of relief. My ribs ached and I knew that I would probably have a massive bruise from the way that he had carried me. I clutched my arms tightly around my rib cage in an attempt to ease the pain.

Slowly he released his grip from my mouth, testing me to see if I was going to scream. I was way too scared and wore out to scream or to try to run. I doubt that it would have done any good out there anyway, so I just stood there. I tried to keep as still as possible while I waited to see what he was going to do next.

Once he was convinced that I was not going to try to take off, he grabbed me by my wrist and started to lead me to the entrance of the cave. This was the first time that I was actually able to get a good look at him. I studied him hard just in case I ever got the chance to go to a police station. I wanted to be able to give them a good description.

He was tall, at least six feet. He was slender but with strong tight muscles that rippled with his movements. His cropped black hair stood out at odd angles on top of his head, and he wore dark blue jeans and a tight fitting black t-shirt. Only when he briefly glanced back at me did I actually get a look at his face. He had the deepest blue eyes that I had ever seen, they were like sparkling sapphires. He had a firm jaw, a straight nose and a small dimple in his chin. He appeared to be clean shaven, but his brows and slight sideburns were black just like his hair.

My goodness those eyes. There was something about his eyes that just seemed to captivate me. Trust me, I knew that they should not appeal to me by any means. Nevertheless, when those eyes locked with mine, it was almost as if I was looking into his soul. What I saw there was a sadness that was maybe mixed with a little remorse. It was almost as if he was pleading with me.

Why would he look sad? That was crazy, he just kidnapped me and was about to do god knows what with me in a cave in the woods.

But his eyes were definitely trying to tell me something. In any other circumstance, I might have thought he was pretty attractive, but right now, I was way too scared and a little to weary to think about him like that.

He had to duck his head as he led me through the narrow opening of the cave. Once we were inside, I could barely see anything. It smelled of damp stale air as I drew in a breath trying to calm myself down. The dankness of the cave began to settle over me and I started to shiver. I was dressed for bed, so I was barefoot and only wearing a pair of comfy pajama bottoms and a thread bare t-shirt. I struggled in the overwhelming darkness to keep my footing as he pulled me forward. He must have sensed my struggle because I felt him slow and then stop. He released my hand and said the first and only word that I had heard him say throughout this entire ordeal. "Stay."

His voice was deep and smooth like velvet. It came across me in a way that made me feel all warm and tingly. I had to shake myself back to reality. What was my problem? This guy was about to torture me to death and I was swooning. Good grief.

I felt him move away from me and I just stood there very still in the dark, shivering. I could not run away if I wanted to because in the pitch black of the cave, I could no longer make out the entrance that we had just walked through only moments before. I heard a rustling noise in the distance and then a moment or two later a soft golden glow began to emit from somewhere out in front of me.

I saw a silhouette coming towards me and before I could blink, he was back and he had me by my wrist once again. He pulled me gently toward the light, slowing occasionally to help me over some rocks or debris.

"What do you want with me?" I managed to choke out. He did not say another word. He just led me through a tunnel off the back of the cave. It had slick, inky walls with jagged edges that scraped and tore at my skin as I was led through it.

I let out an "oomph" as a sharp point gouged into my right bicep. I tried to fight back the tears that wanted to spill out of my eyes. I did not want him to think that I was weak.

He stopped again. I think that he was looking at me, though I could not even tell because of the darkness. "Almost there." He said in that rich velvety voice.

"Uh huh," was all that I could manage to stammer out. First, it was his eyes and now it was his voice. Maybe he had drugged me or something. Why else would I be acting like such a complete idiot? I should be fighting for my life, not drooling over the guy.

We moved forward through the tunnel and it finally opened up to reveal a vast cavern. I noticed a small fire burning in a makeshift pit in the middle of the floor.

Close to the walls of the room it appeared that he had stowed a few supplies. There were a couple of old blankets tossed about, and a worn dark green backpack was leaning against the wall in one corner. He must have been planning this for a while.

"What are we doing here? What is going on?" I demanded.

This time he spoke in a low desperate tone. "I am taking you home."

I jerked my head up to look at him. I squinted my eyes as confusion settled over my face. "What are you talking about? You just ripped me from my home!" I yelled.

He held my gaze for a moment with those eyes. Then as if I had not asked anything at all, he turned away. He began to gather some of the old blankets from across the room. He spread them out on the floor close to the fire.

"Here. Sleep. We still have a long way to go to before we can get you home and you need to rest."

I just looked at him in bewilderment. Slowly a single tear started to make its way down my cheek, betraying my fear. He reached out as if he were going to wipe it from my face, but I jerked away and shrank back from him.

"What do you want from me?" I said in whisper. "Just take me back to my house, please. You do not have to do this."

He looked into my eyes pleadingly. It was almost as if tears started to well up around his own sapphire blues. Why did he always look so sad? He is the one that did this to me! I just could not understand.

"Callie, please." He sounded desperate. "I am trying to bring you home. To your true home. Where you belong. Please do not be so afraid of me. I would never hurt you."

How did he know my name? Was he some sort of deranged stalker?

"Who are you?" I demanded.

"Callie, you know me. You must remember. You must feel it." He pleaded.

I am not sure what he was talking about, but the truth is that I did feel something. I did not know how to explain it, but it was as if I were drawn to him. I really could not even be afraid of him, or even that angry with him, although I should be.

"All that I know is that you kidnapped me from my bed in the middle of the night. Now you have me here in this cave." I gestured at the space around me. "You are probably about to do god knows what kind of evil things to me. You know my name and now you are telling me that I should know you, when I have never seen you before in my life!" I yelled.

I wrapped my arms tightly around myself as if I were trying to keep myself together. He moved toward me, and this time when he reached for me, I did not move away. What would be the point?

He wrapped his long arms around my shoulders and pulled me into an embrace. My cheek rested against his chest and he put his chin on the top of my head as he spoke.

"This will all be clear to you soon. I know that you are afraid of me, but I would never hurt you. It is my duty to protect you, Callie. I will protect you until my last breath. I swear to you. Please Callie, come and rest. Tomorrow you will see. Tomorrow things will be better."

He pulled me down onto the blankets and I let him. What else was I supposed to do? He held me there, wrapped tightly in his strong arms. I breathed in deeply, he smelled so good. He smelled of earth and pine, mixed with something sweet, like honeysuckle.

Despite my fears and frustration, exhaustion overcame me. The warmth of his arms, the sound of his heartbeat, and his scent filling my nose were all more than any girl would be able to handle. Before I knew it, I was fast asleep.

2

I woke to find that I was still lying on the blankets on the floor of the cavern. My captor was no longer lying next to me. I felt a strange longing deep inside of me for him. Maybe it was just fear. Like the fear of realizing that I was alone in the darkness of the cave and far away from home. I rolled onto my back to look around, but he was not there.

The fire still burned but it was starting to fizzle out. I glanced toward the ceiling only to realize that it must have been really tall, because all that I could see in the glow of the fire was darkness.

Sitting up was difficult. My ribs ached from being clutched so tightly for so long the day before. I struggled to get to my feet. I had no idea what time it was but my stomach was definitely growling at me.

"Hello?" I called quietly into the darkness, but all that I heard in return was my echo.

I was not sure what I should do, but I knew that I needed to do something.

I searched the cavern walls until I spotted the entrance and slowly I walked through it and out into the tunnel.

The darkness of the tunnel was disorienting and I thought hard trying to retrace my steps from the day before. I walked a little at a time with one hand trailing gently across the rocky wall.

I stumbled and nearly lost my balance when I stubbed my toe on an outcrop of rock. I cried out briefly, sending echoes of my stunted scream throughout the darkness. The pain shot through my foot and up my leg. A dull throbbing settled into my big toe. I slid down the wall onto my butt on the cold floor, clutching my foot.

How far did I really think that I was going to go with no shoes? I was leaned back against the cool stone waiting for the throbbing in my toe to pass when I heard a low rumbling growl.

I froze, not even wanting to breathe. The growling echoed around the cave walls and slowly seemed to be getting closer. It felt as if it were right in front of me and getting more ferocious.

I clamped my eyes shut tightly, afraid of what I might see if I opened them.

Suddenly, I felt what I was sure was the creature's hot breath on my face. I could smell the rot and decay of its last meal filling my nostrils. I wanted to gag at the thought of it.

Fear ripped through me. All that I could think about was that I was about to be ripped apart by some crazed animal in a cave, in the middle of I had no idea where, and no one would ever be able to find me.

"Callie!" The sound of my name rang loudly in my ears and I flinched for fear that I was about to be torn to shreds. The noise must have distracted the beast because he turned away from me to see who was making such a commotion.

"Callie!" I heard again. Then, all that I could see was the flash of a blade as it sunk down into the animals back. There was a grotesque crunching sound and then a gurgling as it fell onto its side with a thud. Soon it was flying across the tunnel away from me. I continued to hear a lot of loud strange noises, mostly grunts and slashing.

All of a sudden, my captor was bent over in front of me. He was frantically searching my body for any sign of injury.

His face was smeared with blood, and fear had shown brightly in his eyes. He grabbed my face in his blood soaked hands and stared into my eyes.

"Callie." He said in a trembling voice.

"I'm alright." I said breathlessly as he pulled me to my feet and wrapped me tightly in an embrace.

"I am so sorry that I left you like that, Callie. I knew that you would need some food when you woke up and I went out to find something for you to eat. I should never have left you alone. Callie, I hope that you can forgive me." He said in a shaky voice as he buried his face in the crook of my neck and wrapped his hands with my hair.

I could feel him trembling as he held me. We stayed there like that for several minutes. I could not imagine how one minute he could be a crazed kidnapper and the next be so sweet and vulnerable. What was with this guy? I needed some answers and I needed them now.

"Please, tell me who you are." I whispered into his ear as his head was still pinned to my shoulder. "I just do not understand what is happening to me. At least tell me what your name is." I pleaded.

He lifted his head and those pleading blue eyes locked with mine again. He reached up and embraced my face in both of his hands. For just a second, I thought maybe he was about to kiss me. Would it be so bad if he did? I was beginning to think no.

I had never kissed a boy before, but I bet this stranger's kisses would be tender and full of passion. I found myself glancing down at his soft full lips, as I bit my own bottom lip in anticipation.

I had to shake myself so that I would snap back to reality.

"Callie," he whispered. "I'm Brokk. I know that you say that you do not remember me but, you belong to me." I pulled back, raising my eyebrows in shock.

"At least you did once." He said as his head dropped and his chin rested on his chest.

"I do not know you and I do not belong to anybody." My voice was fierce and he looked up again. "You are truly crazy." I whispered.

He dropped his head back down and stared at the floor. He released my face and his arms fell to his sides in defeat.

"Brokk, listen. I don't know why you are doing this, but it's not too late. If you would just take me back home." I pleaded. "I promise that I would never tell anybody or call the police or anything like that. You can go back to where ever you came from and I can forget this ever happened. You do not have to do this."

He just stood there shaking his head as it hung toward the ground.

"We need to get you some food." He said quietly as he pulled himself together and walked away.

I ducked back into the cavern and walked over to warm myself by the few remaining embers in the pit. They were glowing a bright shade of red and snapped and crackled as I stood watching them. I just could not seem to sort out all of the different emotions that were running through my head. I was actually feeling bad for this guy. He looked at me like I was breaking his heart when I talked about wanting to go home. So strange. What was even stranger is that I was not really sure that I wanted to go. At least not without him.

He finally came back to the cavern, his arms were full of wood for the fire, and some sort of meat and what looked like roots. He did not even look at me. I felt a pang of regret rip through me once again. I was compelled to say something. To say anything, just so that he was talking to me again.

"What is all of that?" I asked softly, trying to break the mood.

"Food." He said simply, still not willing to look at me.

I was afraid to ask what kind of food. It was probably some poor forest creature and I was too hungry to think about that right then. I was not sure what else to say so I just stood in silence, watching him.

He set about building the fire back up. It started to blaze beautiful orange and yellows. Once it was burning to his satisfaction, he situated the food around it. The smell of the cooking meat filled the room and smelled wonderful. My mouth was beginning to water as I watched him slowly turning the food from side to side.

I watched him as he kneeled on the floor in the fire light. He never looked back up at me and I wondered what he might be thinking. I still could not shake the feeling that I got when he looked at me. I knew that I should be afraid of him. That is what a normal person would be feeling, but somehow I just was not. I never could be. He could kill me right now and I was not afraid.

I continued to stare at him for a long time. I noticed the rippling of his strong arm muscles as he worked the fire. The way his tight shirt pulled across his rigid chest. The way the fire made is face glow with its warming light. Just watching him like that had my body tingling from head to toe.

I dropped my gaze to the floor. I was embarrassed by what I was thinking and feeling. I should not have been reacting to him like that, but I just could not seem to help myself.

I believed him when he said that he would never hurt me. He had plenty of opportunity to do something if he really wanted and he had not even laid a hand on me.

I thought about the way that he trembled after the animal nearly attacked me, it really had scared him.

What was it about this boy? What did he mean when he said that I belonged to him? He did not even know me, did he?

He keeps saying that I should remember him, but I had no idea what he was talking about. I did not remember anyone like him from school, and I think that I would certainly remember those eyes.

I definitely felt something though. I just did not know how to explain it. Maybe it was just the after effects of the adrenaline in my body from nearly losing my life. That would be enough to scramble anybody's brain, wouldn't it?

Brokk finally turned and stared up at me. I glanced back at him and searched his face for some kind of understanding. It only lasted a moment. It was as if he sensed me looking at him, like I had called to him or something. He met my eyes briefly and then he quickly turned away and went back to preparing the meal.

When he was certain that everything had been cooked enough, he arranged the food on a flat rock and offered for me to come and eat. I was so hungry by then that I did not hesitate. It all smelled so good and I tore into the meat without any delay.

It was heavenly. The savory juices of the meat washed over my pallet and only left me craving more. I looked for Brokk, he had not come to sit with me.

"You are not going to eat?" I asked as he stood a few feet away, watching me.

"I will eat when I am sure that you have had enough." He said with his arms folded across his chest.

"But there is plenty!" I said as I gestured toward the spread of food that he had created. "There is no way that I can eat all of this. Please, come and sit. Plus, I can not take you just standing there staring at me like that."

His mouth started to turn up into a small grin, and he moved toward me. He sat onto the ground on the opposite side of the rock from where I was sitting and began to eat.

The meal was delicious and though Brokk did not say very much his eyes never left me as we ate. I started feeling a little bit self-conscious. I had suddenly remembered that I had not bathed or brushed my teeth, and my hair felt like it was in tangles. I was still in my pajamas from the night before.

I looked down at myself in dismay. I started to rake my fingers through my knotted blonde hair as I scrutinized my now tattered and stained T-shirt and sighed.

"You have grown to be so beautiful, it has been far too long since I have been able to look at you like this." Brokk said in a whisper that made my heart skip a few beats.

I looked up at him, studying him hard in the hope of finding some answers. "Why do you keep talking as if you have known me all of my life? I have tried really hard but I just can't seem to remember you at all."

He looked a little hurt by my comment, but in a hushed voice he answered. "We knew each other when we were very young, before you and your family were forced to flee Petrona."

I stared back at him for a moment.

"How can that be? I was born in Baton Rouge. I have lived my whole life in the house that you took me from. I don't think that I am the girl that you were looking for. I really wish that you could see that and take me back home, back to my real home."

It actually hurt a little to say those words, but it must be true. I never lived anywhere other than my home in Louisiana. I did not even have a clue where in the heck Petrona was.

He looked down briefly. I thought maybe I was starting to get through to him, but then he looked back up and met my eyes.

"I know exactly who you are, Callie Rose. There is no mistaking you. Soon you will see it too. I do not understand why you can't remember me. Maybe it will come to you once I get you back home to Petrona. You are one of us, Callie. Just trust me. All of this will be explained to you soon. They need you there more than you could ever understand."

Those blue eyes pleaded with me once again and I was too mesmerized to think of a decent reply. I opted for nodding my head like an idiot instead. I was turning into a complete loon.

Brokk sat for a few more moments just staring off. Then quickly he said. "We need to be moving. They have been waiting for you to return for a long time."

There he went again. Who was he talking about? He kept saying things like *they* need me and you are one of *us*, like I was supposed to know who he was talking about. Maybe he really was crazy.

He stood and offered me his hand. I took it hesitantly, I was afraid of what touching him might do to me. The last thing that I needed was to have my brain scrambled anymore than it already was. He pulled me to my feet.

He turned to start cleaning up and to put out the fire.

"Wait, I can't go anywhere like this." I said gesturing to myself. "I am not even wearing shoes and the ground here has already done a number on my feet."

"Then I will carry you." He answered without looking up.

"No way!" I said holding my hands up and taking a step backwards. "I am already going to have major bruises from the way that you carried me yesterday! You are not about to do that again!"

He furrowed his brow and stepped towards me hesitantly.

"I never meant to hurt you Callie. Please, let me have a look to be sure that your injuries are not serious. I promise, I am not going to harm you further."

He held my eyes with his and against my better judgment, I found myself wanting to trust him again. I began lifting my shirt just enough to expose my sore and aching ribs.

"Oh no! What have I done!" He gasped as he collapsed to the floor on his knees in front of me. He held out his hands as if he wanted to touch me, but stopped as if he were afraid that he might hurt me more. I looked down at myself to see a dark purple band spread across my entire lower chest. No wonder I was so sore.

"I'm okay, really. It is just a little uncomfortable, but I do not think that I could spend another day traveling like that." I shrugged.

He looked down at my bare feet for a moment, then picked up the blankets from the ground and began tearing them into long strips. When he was satisfied with his little pile of scraps, he nodded to himself and turned to me.

"Sit." He said and so of course, I did. He took my feet into his lap and started to wrap the strips of torn blanket around each foot like huge bandages.

When he was finished, he helped me back onto my feet. It was a bit awkward, but I could stand and walk if I leaned on him for support. He cautiously led me out of the cavern and back into the tunnel. It was slow going with my mummy feet. Plus, I was back in the complete darkness again. I could not see two inches in front of me, so of course, I tripped and stumbled over every little bump.

I started thinking that maybe Brokk was enjoying my handicap a little more than he thought that he would. Each trip over a rock sent me farther into his arms and he held me even tighter.

"Why are we going further into the cave?" I asked as I began to notice that we still had not made it back outside. "I thought we were going to that Petrona place?"

"We are going to Petrona, Callie." He said. "It is beneath the surface. These tunnels will lead us there." I stopped, pulling him back towards me.

"What do you mean beneath the surface?" I made little quote marks in the air with my fingers and mocked him. "Like underground? Are you telling me that you are taking me to a city that is under the ground? Like as in the Land of the Lost or something?"

He just laughed. "Something like that I guess. Callie, our people were forced to move underground. It was many years ago, after living in the upper world became too dangerous for us."

He did it again. He said *our people,* as in something other than people, people. I thought back about how strong he must have been to be able to carry me for as long as he did. Plus he was so fast. I knew that he was not your average teenage guy, but what was he talking about?

"Brokk, what is going on? I have never heard of any underground city." This was getting crazier by the minute. "Where are you taking me and who are you exactly?"

He let out a long sigh, and finally he began. "We are going to the true city of your birth. We are going to Petrona, the home of our people. The Fae, Callie."

Okay, this boy has really lost his mind. "The Fae? As in fairy? Are you trying to tell me that you are a fairy? That *we* are fairies? That *I* am a fairy? Is this some kind of joke?" I started looking around for movie cameras.

He just stood there watching me for a few moments while I let all of what he said sink in.

"You are crazy." I exclaimed. "You kidnapped me and brought into some strange underground tunnels, and now you are talking about fairies as if they truly exist. Is there some kind of dungeon or torture chamber down here that you are taking me to? Are you some kind of psychotic serial killer?"

He moved towards me and caught one of my hands in each of his. "Callie please, I know this must sound strange to you right now, but I am telling you the truth. I was sent to the surface by Queen Lilith to find you. She has been the acting queen since your family left. There has been talk of a revolt by some of the other Fae. She thinks that if she has a true heir to the throne to assist her, then she may be able to bring peace back to our people."

I took a deep breath as I tried to understand all of this. "A true heir? Acting queen? What are you saying Brokk?"

He growled in frustration. "You Callie. You are the true heir. Your mother was queen when you were born, but a group of rogue Fae attempted to kidnap you. They were trying to force the queen to change some of the rules that were preventing them from coming to the surface and harming the humans. Your mother and father decided to take you away and hide with you until you were old enough to return and reclaim your title for yourself."

"There was an old Fae woman." He continued. "Some believed that she could foretell the future. She told your mother that you would someday become a great ruler to our people and that you would lead us out of the darkness and back to the surface where we can be free. After the rebels were stopped, your mother feared that others would try to harm you to get to her. That is when she gave up her throne and fled with you. It took me a long time to find you Callie, and now that I have, you can take your rightful place as the future queen. You are the chosen one, Callie. The one to free us all."

He looked at me again with those pleading blue eyes, but I could not help but laugh. "You actually believe all of this." I said. "You think that I am some chosen one, who is a fairy and supposed to save the world."

"I am just a normal eighteen year old girl, Brokk. I live in a normal house. I go to a normal school. I do not have any super powers, and I am definitely not the savior of your people. My mother is not some fairy queen, she is just my mom. She cooks me dinner and helps me with my homework. My dad works for the phone company. He likes watching football and going fishing and hunting on his days off. He is not a king."

He just shook his head. "Please Callie. Just trust me. Just come to Petrona with me and you can see for yourself that what I am saying is the truth." He held out his hand to me. "Please Callie."

What choice did I really have? He was not about to take me back home, there was no convincing him. I could not find my own way back, even if I really wanted to.

I still wasn't sure what I really wanted anymore. All that I knew is that my heart and my body wanted to be wherever Brokk was going be. I nodded sheepishly at him and took his hand. He began to lead me further into the tunnels.

3

It felt like we had walked for hours through the inky blackness of the tunnel. My makeshift slippers were beginning to fray and come loose. I did not think that I was going to be able to make it another step. I sat down on a large rock.

Brokk turned and saw me struggling to wind the scraps of fabric back around my feet. "Let me carry you the rest of the way. I promise that I will be more careful this time. We can get there a lot faster if I can run."

I made a grimace as I thought about that. "Why do you seem to have all of these super powers, while I can barely walk in a straight line without falling on my face? I thought I was supposed to be some kind of fairy princess?"

He smiled and I swooned. He really did not smile nearly enough. "I do not have super powers really. I have been training for this position all of my life. You will master some of the same things with practice."

He reached for me and scooped me up, cradling me in his arms. "Hold on tight." He said with a laugh and took off running with blinding speed.

We ran through the darkness of the tunnel for some time. His grip on me never faltered.

I kept my face buried in his chest to block my eyes from the wind. I drank in his manly scent and it set my head spinning. I could really get used to this, I thought.

"Look Callie." He said as I felt him start to slow.

I lifted my head and looked out at an enormous city built within a large hollow beneath the earth. I could hardly believe my eyes. There were twinkling lights strung along the rocky streets. Every street was lined with elaborate buildings. Some of them appeared to be homes. They were mostly wooden one or two story structures. Each had been painted with dark shades of either blue, red, or green. Every one had a couple of quaint little windows and a door made of heavy yellow wood.

The businesses were made of both wood and brick. The wooden storefronts were also painted in bright colors. Over the top of each large glass door was an elaborate sign bearing the store's name and what they offered. The merchants had all sorts of food and wares proudly displayed in large glass windows. It was just as I had always imagined that New York City might have looked two-hundred years ago.

I could hear children laughing and playing somewhere close by. I took a deep breath and drank in the delicious aroma of fresh brewed coffee and baked goods. Fairies drink coffee? Who knew?

We made our way down what appeared to be the main street through the city. People, fairy people I assumed, stepped out of their shops and homes to watch us as Brokk carried me passed them. He just nodded to them here and there as we went by. For the most part, I kept my face buried in his shirt. I did not want anyone to see me looking so rough. I was starting to feel a little embarrassed.

I glanced up to see Brokk looking at me. "We need to make a quick stop." He said softly in his smooth sexy voice.

He turned down a small side street that was lined with little wooden homes and stopped in front of one that was painted sapphire blue. How fitting, I thought to myself as I stared up at his eyes. My new favorite color.

Brokk stood me up on my feet on front of the large yellow door. A small sign painted gold off to the right was inscribed with the name Lucerne and the number twenty-three in black lettering.

"Is this your house?" I asked, looking around. He smiled slightly and nodded in affirmation as he used a key to unlock the door. "Your name is Brokk Lucerne?"

"Yes, Callie Rose, that is my name." He sounded amused, but he said nothing more as he pushed the door open and gestured for me to go in.

The inside of his home was warm and cozy, just like I would have imagined it to be. The small living room was neatly decorated with dark brown sofas and shiny black tables. There were a few books scattered on the coffee table and several framed photos hanging on the walls.

The photos were mostly done in black and white. They contained pictures of a happy looking family with two young children, a boy and a girl. "Is this you?" I asked, pointing to the young boy.

"Yes." He grinned as he stared at the photo. "And that is you." He pointed to the young girl in the picture. I flinched and looked from him back to the photo. The girl appeared to be about five or six years old. She was wearing a long flowered dress and her hair was done up in braided pigtails. The two children smiled happily at each other as they ran hand in hand and played in a field of wild flowers.

It really did look like me. I could not deny it. The boy in the picture looked familiar too. I was not sure if it was because I remembered him as a child or because he so closely resembled Brokk as a man.

"We looked so happy." I murmured and then I turned to face him. "What were we doing that day?"

"My parents had taken us to the surface. They thought that we needed to experience as much of the human world as possible. They wanted us to experience the sunshine and the fresh air." He smiled, mostly to himself I think.

"So we visited the surface regularly?" I asked.

"Pretty often." He replied. "It was one of the advantages of being a royal at the time. Most of the Fae never get to see the sun anymore. They spend their whole lives down here. Only a select few get to go up there now. Mostly just merchants and occasionally a guard can go, if needed."

It must have been really hard to spend so much time underground. I had only been there for a few days and I was already missing the sun. Not only that but also the flowers and the trees, and the feel of the breeze on a hot summer day. All of the things that people normally take for granted.

"Why did you have to stop? Why can't anyone go up there now?" I asked.

"Well, once Lilith took control she made it a law. I am not really sure why, but if you are caught going without permission there are major consequences. Some have been jailed or even killed."

"Killed?" I was shocked. "Why would she kill someone?"

"She did not want your parents alerted to what was going on here. If they were to return, she would lose her status. So she considered anyone caught trying to pass any information on to them to be a traitor." He looked grave.

"Then why would she want me here?" If she did not want my parents to know what she was up to, you would think that the last thing that she would want was for me to be here.

Brokk stood in silence for a moment. "Her plan was to show the people that she is willing to work with you. She would still be in power but she would be willing to take you under her wing and prepare you for when you take the thrown."

"This all seems a little crazy. Obviously, my parents are going to wonder where I am. They are going to come looking for me. I can't possibly stay here. " I started pacing the small room.

"Maybe, but I think that she was hoping that they would allow you to stay here if they knew that she was getting you ready to take control." He said.

That seemed a little far-fetched to me too. I don't know why but everything about this situation left me feeling uneasy. I had never even heard of these people or anything about being a queen or princess, or whatever. Now I was supposed to just give up my life and stay here, far away from everything that I knew and loved? I just did not think that I could do that.

"Brokk, even if you are right. Even if my parents think that is okay for me to be here, I don't know if it is even something that I want." I began. "I had a life. I was about to graduate. I was supposed to start college in the fall. I never even wanted to be a princess when I was a little girl. I wanted to ride horses and roll around in the dirt. This just isn't for me."

He moved toward me then and held me in place by my left bicep as he looked me in my eyes. "Callie, Petrona was always meant to be yours. You were born here, your parents were born here. There is not another place on this earth that is more for you than right here."

The tension in my body grew to a palpable level, and not because of all of the talk about queens and kingdoms. Brokk's eyes bore into me with such intensity that I felt myself drifting towards him without any effort at all. I stopped thinking about cities and tunnels. I became solely focused on the way that his mouth moved when he talked and I completely lost myself in his eyes. I couldn't even speak.

"Callie?" His faced changed to something close to worry.

I snapped myself out of it. "Sorry." I said as I felt my blood rush to my cheeks in an instant and embarrassing blush. I must have really zoned out for him to react like that. "Maybe I better sit down for a little while."

I had to do something to distract myself from wanting to pounce on him every time that he looked at me.

Brokk directed me over to one of the couches. It was plush and comfortable. I sank down into it and started to relax. He went into one of the rooms toward the back of the house while I waited.

When he emerged, he was carrying a small cardboard box. He sat down on the couch a few feet away, but he propped his back against the armrest so that he was facing me. He stared down at the box for a few minutes, he seemed hesitant to open it. When he finally did, he held out a ring to me.

The ring was gorgeous. The center stone was a large square sapphire that perfectly matched the color of his eyes. I was not sure which sparkled more, the stone or Brokk's eyes as he held it out to me. The sapphire was surrounded by several tiny diamonds and even more ran around the platinum band.

"Brokk?" I was speechless once again.

"Callie, I know that you have only known me for a short time but you and I were meant to be together. Not just because our families arranged for us to be married, but because we are so strongly linked to each other. You must feel it. I know that I do." He said.

I just sat there looking at him. The truth was, I did feel it. It was hard to explain, but I was drawn to him. Even under the most dire circumstances, I could not fight it.

When I did not speak right away, he continued. "This ring belonged to my mother. She had always hoped that you and I would be together once you returned. She gave this to me just before she passed away. She always wanted you to have it."

He took my hand in his and slid the ring onto my finger. "I know that it is too soon for us to make any real promises to each other, but it would really mean a lot to me if you would wear it. It was always meant to be yours, and so was I."

I did not know if I was going to laugh or cry but I suddenly felt tears spring up in my eyes. "Brokk, I don't even know what to say. It is so beautiful."

"You do not have to say anything. I just wanted you to have it." He said nervously.

"Thank you." I flung my arms around his neck. "I will never take it off." I said softly into his ear.

He pulled me even closer so that he held me in his lap and wrapped his arms tightly around me, burying his face in my hair. He held me as if he never wanted to let me go.

We stayed curled up together in his couch for what seemed like hours. Neither of us really spoke, we just savored the feeling of being so close to someone.

Our moment was interrupted by a sharp knock at the door. Brokk rose to answer it. I could hear him speaking sharply to someone outside. When he was through, he returned to the living room looking very grim.

"Is everything okay?" I asked.

"The queen has sent her guards to see if we have returned. She is expecting you at the palace shortly." He frowned.

I nodded. "Okay, I think that I am as ready as I will ever be."

He took me by the hand and pulled me to my feet. He stopped just before opening the door and hugged me tightly for a few more moments. Then we stepped out onto the darkened street.

4

Brokk cradled me in his arms again and I savored the closeness as he carried me.

The shops along the main street of the city were beginning to close up for the evening. The merchants were all busy pulling their wares inside and they did not seem to notice us as we passed.

I could not help but to be distracted by the weight of the heavy ring that now occupied my left hand. I smiled to myself as I looked down at it and imagined all the possibilities it could mean for my future. I just did not think that my future would be here.

Brokk was great, even if he did kidnap me, but I longed to be back home in Louisiana. Maybe I could convince him to go with me. We could have a normal life, and live in a normal house. I could finish school and see my family again. I would just have to convince the queen that she did not need me here and that I had no intention of taking over.

We neared the end of the street and made our way up several steps and to the front of an enormous palace. It was pristine white, a sharp contrast from the darkness of the rest of the city. On either end was a pointy roofed turret with little rectangular windows on each side.

In the center was a grand arched doorway with marble steps that jutted out into a semi-circle. It was beautiful.

The yard surrounding the palace was lush and green, and there was an ornate wrought iron fence encircling it. There were even flowers and shrubs lining the walls. It was actually a pretty odd site considering that the sun never reached this area.

We approached the door and Brokk set me on my feet in front of it. "This is your true home, Callie. This is where you belong."

"This is it? We are going inside now? I can't go inside of there looking like this!" I frantically whispered.

"You will be fine Callie. The Fae that work here will take care of you. They will make sure that you get a proper bath, and something to eat before you meet with the queen. You are where you were always meant to be now."

He said these words, but a deep sadness was clearly audible in his voice. He started stepping back down the stairs.

Was he leaving? What was going on?

I glanced back at him. "Does this mean that you are not coming with me?" I asked.

"This is your home, Callie, not mine. You will be fine." He said with a smile that did not quite reach his eyes.

"This is not my home either Brokk, remember? I do not want to go in there without you." I hissed.

Ignoring me, he stepped forward and knocked on the door with a huge ornate knocker. A tiny window perched at eye level flew open and a pair of bright green eyes peered out through the opening. It was quickly slammed shut again.

There was a bit of a commotion on the other side of the entrance and finally the large door was opened. A small girl who appeared to be about my age was standing in front of us. She was wearing a simple black dress and her reddish brown hair was pulled up into a loose curly bun on top of her head. She had the same green eyes that I spotted peering through the small window.

"Brokk?" She looked at him in surprise.

"Bree, this is Callie. The queen is expecting her. Callie, I would like you to meet Bree. She lives here too and I know that she will make sure that you have everything that you need."

He turned back to Bree and said. "Thank you Bree, call on me if you need anything more from me." Bree nodded and he looked back to me, his eyes seemed to search my face for something.

"I will take my leave now." He said simply.

"Please, do not leave me here Brokk. Why do you refuse to stay with me? I do not want to go in there without you." I pleaded with tears in my eyes.

He looked again at Bree and she gestured with her head for him to go, and he did. He turned and ran back down the steps and into the city streets. He never looked back.

I watched him leave until he disappeared behind some buildings. I did not understand why, but my heart felt like it was breaking in two and tears threatened to spill from my eyes. I turned back to Bree.

"Well." She said shaking her head. "That was interesting."

"Follow me. We need to get you cleaned up before Queen Lilith knows that you are here. We can't have her seeing you looking like some sort of street urchin." She said as she breezed through the doorway.

I followed her inside of the house and into a grand sitting area. The floors were a polished white marble and there were cozy cream colored sofas arranged about the room on fuzzy white carpets. Huge paintings adorned the walls and colorful flower arrangements were scattered about on tables.

A large staircase fanned out into the center of the room, and I followed Bree up the stairs and to the left down a long hallway. She stopped in front of a white door that was ornately trimmed in gold.

"This is going to be your room." She said as she opened the door and walked inside.

I followed her in and my mouth gaped open at the gorgeous interior. There was a large white four poster bed that was draped in beautiful flowing white netting.

The bedding and pillows were also white and they were trimmed in a delicate eyelet lace. The comforter looked especially cozy, like big white clouds of fluff.

I definitely could not wait to sleep in that glorious bed, especially after the last few nights that I had.

The walls were painted a beautiful blue, like the color of the sky. Ornate French doors led out onto a large marble balcony that overlooked the city. I turned to see Bree emerge from a large walk-in closet carrying a long flowing coral colored gown.

"Come on lets get you into the tub." She said as she walked through yet another door and into a beautiful private bath with a large tub built into the wall.

Once again, everything appeared to be made of shiny white marble. The only difference is that in my bathroom everything was trimmed in pink. There were fuzzy pink carpets scattered about the floor, pink towels, and even a vase a fragrant pink roses on the counter of the long sink.

Bree ran the water and filled the tub with bubbles that smelled like fresh lilacs and then she turned to me. "Well come on, climb in."

"You are not leaving?" I asked as I hugged my arms across my ragged t-shirt.

"No Callie, my job is to take care of you." She huffed. "If you insist on being shy, I will turn my back until you can get undressed and into the tub." She turned to face the wall.

Okay, so apparently she was not going budge on this so I quickly slipped out of my torn and tattered pajamas and slid into the water. The bath felt heavenly after being in the cold dank tunnels for nearly two days. I think it was days, or maybe it was nights. I was losing track of the time here without being able to see the sun.

Bree turned around and gathered up my discarded garments. "I am sending these out to be burned." She said as she tossed them into a small trash bin.

I laid back in the bath and felt the warmth of the water washing away all of my stress and fatigue, but only for a moment. As soon as I got comfortable, Bree came over to the tub. She took my arm and began to scrub me from head to toe.

"Bree!" I tried to protest, but she just shook her head and gave me a stern look.

"I have to be sure that you are perfectly clean or I have to answer to the queen, so just sit back and let me do my job Callie!" She was starting to sound exasperated.

Believe me when I say that Bree took her job very seriously. I was beginning to wonder if I would have any skin left at all by the time that she was through with me.

When she was satisfied that my skin was squeaky clean, she moved on to thoroughly shampooing my hair. She clipped and trimmed my fingernails and then my toe nails too.

She helped me to dry off, completely disregarding my protests. When she was finally finished, I had my long blonde hair arranged around my head in ringlets, and just a touch of pretty make up on my face that made my skin seem to shimmer. She applied dark mascara that made my soft brown eyes stand out against my glowing tan skin.

She helped me slip into the gown that she had picked out and slid a pair of matching little slippers onto my feet that reminded me of when I was a little girl in ballet class. That memory hit me hard. How could I have been in ballet class as a little girl when I was supposed to have lived here?

"There," she said snapping me out of my reverie. She gave me a once over and nodded her final approval. "Now you are presentable enough to go and meet the queen."

"Right now?" I had no idea that I would have to meet her so soon. My palms started to sweat and I could barely contain my nerves.

"Callie, pull yourself together!" Bree hissed.

"I am trying." I grumbled.

Bree grabbed me by the hand and led me from my room. We walked back down the stairs and past the sitting area, into a formal dining room.

The walls were painted in an elaborate gold design. Large framed paintings of sunny meadows and other landscape scenes were meticulously placed about the walls. A long crystal chandelier hung suspended from the ceiling by a thick gold chain.

There was a long table that must have seated at least twenty people. It was made of a dark wood that had been polished until it shined like glass. In the center of the table was an enormous flower arrangement that had to be at least four feet long and three feet high. It was loaded with colorful spring flowers and roses of nearly every shade imaginable.

Sitting at the far end of the table was a tall slender woman, with sharp blue eyes and a sharp nose to match.

Her coal black hair was pulled up in a tight twist. She attempted to smile at me but her smile never quite made the upward curve.

"Your highness." Bree said with a bow. "I present to you Miss Calliope Rose."

I did sort of a half bow, half curtsey kind of thing. I had no idea what the appropriate gesture should be. The queen signaled for me sit down into one of the cushioned high back chairs at the table. Once I was seated, Bree disappeared and I was left sitting there alone with the queen eyeing me up like I was some sort of criminal.

"Miss Rose, how delighted we are to have you here." The queen said with much sarcasm and an icy glare.

"T-thank you," I stammered. Why was she acting so cold if she is the one who sent for me to begin with? This whole thing just was not making any sense.

"I take it your parents are doing well?" She asked, but still with a smirk on her face.

"Yes, they are fine, thank you." I said. "How do you know my parents?"

"We are old friends." She said as she waved off my question as if it was of no importance.

A man dressed in a dark suit brought two bowls of creamy looking soup on a tray and set one bowl in front of each of us. I waited until the queen tasted hers and then my stomach could not stand it any longer and I started to eat mine too. It was delicious and I savored every bite until the man returned and collected our bowls.

We went on that way through several more courses. The next dish that came out was a salad of mixed leafy greens and cucumbers. Then a plate filled with roasted chicken and vegetables. At least I hoped that it was chicken. I wondered where they got all of the food and flowers. I had not seen any farms, and without sunlight how would anything grow? Very strange.

We mostly ate in silence. Occasionally, I would look up to see the queen glaring at me. I would always look away again quickly. She was really beginning to rattle my nerves.

Halfway through the dessert, which put me in mind of a rich and yummy key lime pie, the queen turned and looked at me sternly.

"I hope that you do not think that you are going to just come sauntering back into Petrona and take over my rein, because prophecy or no prophecy, I am still the queen."

I dropped my fork and looked up to meet her eyes. "I did not ask to come here. You sent for me. You sent Brokk to search for me and you had him snatch me from my home in the middle of the night to bring me here. If you did not want me here, then why didn't you just leave me where I was?"

"The people of Petrona were starting to get restless." She explained as she lifted her chin. "They started asking for Queen Faylinn and talking about all of the stuff that the foolish old woman told your mother. I brought you here to show my subjects that I am willing to listen to their requests. So that they may be appeased, but you will not get in my way, is that understood?"

I nodded. I had no idea what to say. I wanted to tell her exactly what I thought that she could do with herself, but then I thought better of it.

"You will be presented to the people of Petrona. There will be a ball in your honor, and you will make a few visits to town here and there, for appearances only."

"You will not speak unless spoken to, and you will keep those conversations to a minimum. Other than that, I do not want you anywhere in sight. Theirs or mine. Is that clear?"

I just stared at her in shock.

"I said is that clear?" She growled and I flinched.

"Y-yes, your majesty. I understand." I managed to get out.

"Good." She replied. "Now get out of here. I do not want to see you again unless I call for you." She rolled her eyes slightly and turned away.

I stood up from the table on very shaky legs and Bree hurried in to get me. We barely made out into the sitting area before I started to cry. I could not help it. They stress of the last few days just came crashing down on my shoulders.

"Come on." Bree urged. "We need to get you to your room before she hears you."

Bree rushed me up the stairs and into my room. I fell onto the bed, buried my face into the comforter, and sobbed as she shut and locked the door.

"Callie, everything is going to be okay. You will just do what she asks and we will try to keep you out of sight when she is around."

I turned to face her and sat up. "I did not ask to come here Bree! I did not want any of this! Now I am just supposed to forget about my life and my family to sit here locked away in this room until she wants to use me as her little puppet!

It is just not fair! I will not do it! I am leaving as soon as I can find Brokk and get him to take home." I sobbed.

"Callie." Bree said gently. "Brokk is a guard for the queen. If he goes against her wishes, she will kill him."

I definitely was not looking to get anyone killed, especially Brokk. There was something about him that I just could not wrap my mind around. I looked down at the deep blue stone that hung from my finger. It reminded me of his eyes and I found myself wishing that I were with him right then.

I knew that I had to stay, especially if the queen would hurt Brokk. I would do what I had to in order to protect him. Despite the whole kidnapping thing, he had always been very sweet to me and I could not deny the feelings that I was having for him.

"I just don't know what else to do." I said.

"You just do what she asks until we can figure something else out." Bree said.

5

The next week was spent in my room, literally. I even ate in my room. The only time that I left my room was to stand out on the balcony and watch the busy people go about their daily lives in the city. When I was out on the balcony, I always found myself searching the faces on the street for Brokk. I could not believe that I had been here for this long and he had not made any effort to see me.

I know that taking care of me was just part of his job, but I could have sworn that we had more of a connection than that. Why else would he have given me his mother's ring. It just did not make any sense.

Maybe I had driven him away with all of my whining about going home. Whatever was happening, all that I know is that it has left me feeling very hollow and alone.

Bree turned out to be my only contact with the outside world. She came in bright and early every morning with my breakfast. She helped me to dress and bathe, and she stopped back in periodically throughout the day to bring me meals or to check up on me.

I spent most of my day reading or napping. The only problem with that is that I was awake during most of the night. That is when the loneliness and despair really set in. I could hardly bare it sometimes.

I tried to leave a few times. Only to find that I was locked inside of my room, of course. I was not even allowed to go to the kitchen or sitting area. I was a prisoner in every sense of the word.

I worried about what my parents must have been thinking and feeling. I felt sure that they were upset. They probably had an idea of where I was, but I bet they are wondering if that is a good thing or not.

I had truly expected them to have come for me by now. The thought of them not looking for me caused me even more heartache. How could they just let me go like that and not even come to check on me?

This morning was no different than all of the rest. Bree came in as she did every morning. She breezed through the door carrying a tray of food. Waffles, fruit, toast, and juice was my breakfast for the day. She flittered about my closet selecting my clothes as I nibbled a piece of toast. "Why do you even bother?" I asked. "I am not going anywhere, so who cares what I am wearing?"

She looked at me and frowned. "Today you are going to town to get fitted for some formal clothes. Therefore, yes I do care about what you are wearing. You need to be clean and ready to go in about an hour."

I had not been able to visit the city since my arrival, so that was pretty exciting news. "You mean that she is letting me out of my cage?" I asked sarcastically.

"Only long enough for me to run a few errands and for you to visit the seamstress, oh and you have to be in disguise." Bree replied.

"I have to wear a disguise?" I asked exasperated.

"Yes, but it should not be that bad. You will just have to wear one of my uniforms and we will tuck your hair up into a tight bun. Oh and you can wear these glasses." She said as she handed me an old pair of black framed glasses.

"They are my grandmother's but she just uses them for reading. Hopefully, nobody will pay much attention to you since they will think that you are just a servant or something."

She went about dressing me, and putting my hair up. By the time that she was through, I barely even recognized myself. I wore one of Bree's black uniform dresses, it was a little snug but it would do. My hair was pulled up in a tight bun on the back of my head, and the dark heavy glasses hid the details of my face.

Bree's disguise was put to the ultimate test as we passed through the sitting area and headed for the door.

"Bree, do not forget to pick up my beads from the jeweler while you are out." Called the queen who was lounging on one of the sofas. She just glanced at me briefly and went back to reading her book without another word.

Bree gave me a quick grin and raised her eyebrows to show me how satisfied she was with her disguise.

We stepped out of the front door and onto the marble steps that led down into the streets of the city. I was so excited to be out of my room that I was nearly bursting. I was bouncing up and down with glee. Bree gave me a stern look and I stopped, pouting a little.

I breathed the air in deeply, it was scented heavily with the smell of baking bread, and I sighed. "Mmm."

"Hush." Bree said. "You are going to draw to much attention to us." Shaking her head, she took me by my arm and led me through the streets of Petrona.

I tried as hard as I could to take in my surroundings. Along the main avenue, there were several clothing stores with beautiful mannequins proudly displaying the style of each store. In one of the windows, I saw an adorable red and white striped top with a flirty black bow off to the side of its scooped neck collar.

"Oh wow, Bree. I want that." I exclaimed, but Bree only ignored my drooling and tugged me along the sidewalk.

I spotted the bakery. It was stacked with cakes, pies, and breads. My mouth was watering as I looked longingly into the window. Each time that I gradually managed to pull away from Bree to check something out, she would pull me back to her and scold me about giving myself away.

It would have been nice if I could have taken more time to browse. It would have been especially nice if I would have had some money to purchase a few of the things that I so desperately wanted or needed. I would have to do something about that.

Maybe I could talk Lilith into letting me work as a housekeeper or something. She would probably enjoy watching me do menial labor. Not that I was above it, but she did not know that. To her I was the princess who was a threat to her crown.

The first stop on my outing with Bree was at the seamstress shop. Sew Lovely was the name of the little place. It was tucked along one of the side streets. The sign hanging over the door depicted a spool of thread and a needle with a long red string hanging from it. A little bell chimed as we entered through the door.

The seamstress introduced herself as Gertrude. She was a sweet older lady with fiery red hair. It was fastened on top of her head by two large knitting needles.

She had the kindest pale blue eyes, and they shined with joy as she talked about her shop and all of the things that she could do.

She measured me from head to toe. When she finished she showed Bree and I several nice fabrics and a few patterns that the queen had requested for my wardrobe. There was lace and satin in every color imaginable.

Apparently, the seamstress was the only person in town that knew my true identity. She took me into a large dressing room and had me try on a very elegant gown. It was silver satin and covered in sparkling rhinestones. I could not wait to see how it looked.

"This one will be for the ball." She said with glee.

"I am going to a ball?" I asked in amazement.

"Oh, why yes dear." She said. "You didn't know? The ball is for you. It is where you will be announced to the whole city."

I remembered the queen mentioning a ball when I had first arrived, but I had been locked away ever since. She never mentioned that it would be so soon. Actually, she had not spoken to me at all since then.

Gertrude went on tucking and pinning the dress to prepare it so that it would properly fit. While tucking one sleeve she leaned in close and whispered. "Child, how are your parents? Will they be coming back to Petrona for the ball?"

I was so shocked that I did not know what to say. "My parents?" I asked.

"Well, yes." She said hesitantly. "Everyone is hoping that they will return and take the throne back from that retched Queen Lilith. Things just have not been the same since she became queen. But please do not repeat what I say. I would hate to lose my head over such a thing. Perhaps I should not have said anything at all."

"No, no. I would never tell. I have no idea what has become of my parents. I miss them terribly. I wish that they were here. They would definitely know what to do about all of this." I said.

I felt another pang of loneliness at the mention of my parents. I wished that I could just go back home. I hated being locked away from everything that I loved. I missed my parents. I missed my home. I even missed Brokk. I stared at the floor as Gertrude finished up my fitting. She kept chatting away but I did not hear another word. I was too lost in my own misery.

I could not help but stare down at my ring. It looked beautiful against the shimmering silver fabric of the dress. I imagined Brokk escorting me to the ball. I bet he would look awesome in a tuxedo. We could spend the whole night dancing in each other's arms. If only I could get to see him again. I would definitely ask him.

As soon as my fitting was finished, Bree rushed me out the door and we continued down the busy street.

She needed to pick up a few things at the market, so we roamed through the carts and stalls that had been set up for the merchants.

There were lots of different farmers there selling everything from cheese to meats to fruit. Bree picked out the few things on her list that the cook had asked her to pick up while I moseyed up and down the aisles taking everything in.

Everyone seemed very friendly. They said hello and smiled as I walked by, I wondered what Gertrude meant when she said that things had not been the same since my parents left.

Bree finished up with her purchases and we turned the corner from the market and headed for the jeweler. As we walked, I noticed a group of men gathered around what looked to be guards. They were dressed in deep navy uniforms with some sort of emblems embroidered on them.

My heart raced as I searched their faces hoping to at least spot a glimpse of Brokk. Just as I was about to give up and turn into the jeweler's shop with Bree, a dark haired guard walked over to join the others. I froze where I was and stared at him as I held my breath. The weight of my stare must have been too much, because he lifted his gaze and searched the crowd until his eyes met mine. We stood there like that for several minutes, not wanting to move or look away.

However, another guard caught his attention and pointed animatedly at some of the men in the crowd.

"Callie, what are you doing? Get in here!" Bree called from inside of the shop and hesitantly I turned and walked inside.

The rest of the day seemed to pass in a fog. I walked with Bree to the remainder of her stops, but I hardly noticed where I was or who I met. My mind was on one person and one person only. Brokk.

I did not know why I was letting him affect me this way. When I was with him all that I had wanted to do was get away from him and get home to my family, but now that he was gone, I longed to see him again.

I could not help but think of those deep blue eyes and the way that they were smoldering at me in the cave. Or of how his arms felt, as he held me until I fell asleep. How could he be so kind one minute, and just walk away the next? Did he have any idea how bad the queen was treating me? No, he could not. He would have come for me if he did. That is what I kept telling myself anyway.

Bree browsed around the shelves of the leather shop on her last stop. The smell of leather was always one of my favorite scents. I stood just outside of the door with my head resting against the glass display window lost in my own thoughts. I felt something brush lightly down my cheek and turned quickly to find Brokk pulling his hand back from my face.

The feeling of warmth and relief that I felt just standing there next to him was almost overwhelming. I thought that I was missing him these last few days, but I had no idea how much until he was right in front of me. I wanted to throw myself onto him and never let him go again, but I did not know if he was feeling the same way.

"Oh." I said, sounding surprised. "Where did you come from?"

He let out a brief chuckle and then went back to looking way to serious. "Callie, what are you doing out here? And why are you dressed as a servant?"

"Brokk." I had no idea where to start, or even if I should. Instead, I asked, "Where have you been? I have not heard a word from you for over a week."

He looked down. "I have had a lot of work to do. It has kept me away from here for a few days." There was something in the tone of his voice that I could not understand. Like he was trying to keep something from me.

"Brokk? Is something wrong?" I asked.

He met my eyes then, and his were swimming with tears that had not yet spilled over as he choked out his words.

"Callie, something terrible has happened. I tried to stop it, but I was too late." He bowed his head again as the tears began to stream down his face.

I grabbed him by his arm and led him around to the back of the building. I had no idea what this was about, but we definitely did not need an audience.

"What is going on Brokk? What has happened? Tell me please."

"They must have followed me when I tracked you." He said in a rush. "After I brought you here, I went back to the surface to check on your parents. I felt sure that they knew that we had come for you, but still, I wanted to be sure that they were okay. Callie, they were not okay. They were not. I am so sorry." He sobbed.

"They were dead." He said the words but they were barely audible.

It took a few moments for his statement to sink in. When it did, it was as if someone had just slapped me hard across the face.

The feelings of shock and despaired ripped through me. I had to place one of my hands against the wall to brace myself. I was not sure that I would be able to stand on my own. My parents. Both of them. Dead?

"How?" Was all that I could manage to say.

"They were murdered, Callie. Their throats had been cut." He whispered.

The scene played out in my mind. The horror of it was almost too much. I did not want to think about it. I tried to look at something else to distract myself, but it was no use. All that I could see was my parents lying on the floor covered in blood.

"Callie, look at me." I heard Brokk say. I pulled myself from my thoughts and looked up to find him staring into my eyes. I searched his face for some answers. I could feel my emotions changing from despair to anger and rage.

"Who? Who did this, Brokk? You said they must have followed you, who followed you?" I demanded in a whisper.

"The guards. The queen's personal guards. I thought it would be enough if she had you. I know that she has always dreaded the return of King Elver and Queen Faylinn. I knew that she was greedy for power, but I never would have thought that she would do something like this." He said desperately.

"What do you mean that you thought it would be enough if she had me? You knew that she hated me? You knew why she brought me here?" I yelled in disbelief. He knew all along what she wanted, and he did not even care. He practically delivered me to her wrapped up in a bow.

I started to shrink back from him. All of the sudden I could no longer stand to be in his presence.

"Callie, please." He pleaded; his tears were still falling from his eyes. "Please let me explain."

"NO!" I cut him off. "Stay away from me! I hate you! I hate your freaking guts! I never want to see your face again!" I screamed as all of my pain and anger boiled to the surface.

I could not stand it anymore. I had to get away from him. I had to get away from everything.

I started to run. I had no idea where I would go, but it did not matter. I had never felt so much pain in my life.

I heard him calling after me.

"Callie! Callie please! Stay!"

I just ignored him and ran faster.

6

I continued to run until I thought my lungs would collapse. All that I could think about was my parents lying in a pool of their own blood. I could not get the image out of my mind.

I ran up and down the streets of the city. I started to fear that I would never find my way out. I ran past endless people that turned to stare. I never stopped. I couldn't.

As I ran, I spotted something that caught my attention. I slowed my pace and finally, I stopped. I bent over with my hand on my side. I was panting for breath and my muscles ached from exhaustion.

I looked around and found that I was alone. I had noticed along one of the walls of the cavern that surrounded the city, that there was a heavy iron door. A shiny gold padlock dangled from it but it was not closed. I stepped forward, ripped the lock from the latch, and carefully slid into the narrow passageway that was behind it. I carefully closed the door behind me.

I vaguely wondered why a locked door would be along the city's wall. I also wondered why it might have been left unlocked, but I could not stop long enough to think about it.

I did not want to be caught somewhere that I was not supposed to be.

I pressed forward through the passageway and it led into large tunnel. It was very much like the one that Brokk had brought me through. The walls were slick and dark, and it smelled of mold and stagnant water. I worried that I might see a rat or something worse.

The one thing that I did not expect was to be able to see as clearly in the dark as I did now. There were no lights or lanterns in this tunnel, the same as before. Only now, I could make out the piles of jagged rocks that were strewn about the floor, and I could see to avoid the sharp edged stones sticking out from the wall. Perhaps spending a week underground with no natural light had caused my eyes to be able to see more clearly in the dark. I had no idea how else to explain it.

I followed the tunnel for a good while through the darkened underbelly of the earth. I had ran for so long in the city that I knew that I would have to rest soon. My legs were starting to ache and I was very winded.

I could barely make out that the tunnel branched off a few yards ahead of me. I made my way to the intersection and stood there contemplating which way to go. I was deep in thought and feeling sorry for myself when I suddenly heard what I thought sounded like music coming from one of the two corridors.

I followed the sound of the music down the corridor to my right. I knew that I had made the correct choice because the sound became louder and louder as I approached. I made my way around a sharp curve and to my amazement, I found that there was another large cavern, almost as large as the one that contained Petrona.

The cavern was filled with the warm glow of fire light, and the scent of a delicious meal cooking on a fire. There were small wooden shacks scattered about, and several people were gathered around a large fire in the center of the village. Some of them danced while others played a little tune with flutes and piccolos.

The music came to a sudden stop. I looked around to see what was happening. I could see that one of the flute players had spotted me and dropped down on one knee into a bow, then gestured for the others to follow suit. They all kneeled and bowed their heads to the ground in the same manner as the first and I just froze where I stood.

"Hello?" I said after a few moments passed.

"My lady." The flute player said as he started to stand.

He looked like he was maybe a few years older than me. He was tall and thick with very powerful looking muscles. He had dark brown hair and a broad smile that filled the room as he beamed at me.

He wore snug fitting blue jeans and an old I love NY t-shirt that was just tight enough to really show off his huge biceps.

"Hi, I am sorry to interrupt," I started to say.

"No, my lady. You did not interrupt." He said. "We were just having a little fun after a long day of work. What brings you down here, if I may ask?"

"It is actually kind of a long story. I was trying to get away from the city and I found this tunnel." I gestured toward the passage behind me. "I really do not mean to intrude."

"You could never intrude, my lady." He replied.

Wow, what was with all of this "my lady" business? No one is supposed to know that I was even here, but this guy is certainly treating me as if I were royalty.

"Do you know who I am?" I asked.

"Oh yes, Princess. I know exactly who you are." He said with a smile.

How could he know me? What if these were the guards that killed my parents? I slowly started to back my way toward the passageway. I needed to get out of there before it was too late.

"We have been waiting for you to return for many years, Princess Calliope." He said as he stepped forward. "When your parents made the decision to leave Petrona for your safety, it was my father and a few others that helped them to escape. My father taught them how to use their glamour to keep themselves hidden away from the humans."

"Glamour?" I asked puzzled.

"Have they not taught you anything of our people since you have been back?" He asked, looking troubled.

"Do not tell me that you are going to start spouting off about fairies too!" I said. "I have heard all that I need to hear about fairies from that jerk, Brokk!"

"Brokk?" He looked startled. "They have introduced you to Brokk?"

"Brokk is who they sent to kidnap me from my home! Brokk is the one that dragged me down here to this awful place! Brokk is the reason that my parents are dead!" I yelled before I could stop myself.

"The King and Queen are dead? No!" He was clearly shaken. The others that were still gathered around him were obviously upset as well. Their whispers increased in intensity and some of them began to weep.

"How could this happen?" He asked.

I explained to him how Brokk had taken me from my home and brought me to the queen. I explained how the queen had locked me away. I told him all of the things that she planned to use me for.

I then had to explain the heartbreaking story that Brokk had told me earlier that day. I told him about how Brokk had found my parents, and about how I ran away and ended up back in the tunnels.

I was thoroughly worn out by the time that I was through. I buried my face in my hands and sobbed until I cried out all of my pent up tears.

"Princess," he said gravely. "You must be exhausted. Come, sit and have dinner with us. We will explain the ways of our people to you, while some of the others go and prepare a place for you to rest."

He led me to a group of chairs that were arranged close to the fire. He had me sit and he propped my feet up on an old wooden box while some of the other villagers finished preparing the meal.

"Thank you." I said. "You are being so kind to me and I do not even know your name."

"You do not need to thank me Princess, you are always welcome here. I apologize for not introducing myself sooner. I am Kailen, and this place is called Drake." He swooped his arm out across the cavern. "The village of the outcasts."

"Outcasts?" I asked.

"Princess, we choose to follow only the true King and the true Queen." He explained. "Lilith is an imposter. We could never live under the rule of a fraud and tyrant such as Lilith. So, when your family left so did we, and most of us settled here, in Drake."

Obviously, I was a little too hasty when I thought that these men might have been among those that killed my parents. They were still very loyal to my family after all of these years.

"Kailen, please call me Callie. I only learned of my parent's true identity a little over a week ago, and I have never thought of myself as a princess." I asked.

"As you wish, Callie." He smiled. "Now tell me, what have you been told about our people?"

I thought for a moment. "Only that we are fairies, and that we were forced to go underground when we started to fear the humans." I said. "Oh, and Brokk kept calling me the *Chosen One*. He mentioned something about a prophecy."

Kailen laughed. "Yes, some do believe in a prophecy. An old fortuneteller spoke of your birth, and your eventual rule here. That is in fact why your mother insisted that she take you away from here to protect you. You are destined to be a very powerful woman, Callie. That news made a few people quite nervous."

"Why? Why would anyone want to stay if I am destined to lead us out of here and back into the world above?" I asked.

"There are many reasons that people would want to stay here." He explained. "Power and greed are a strong force. Someone like Lilith would want to keep you from taking your rightful place as the queen. She is quite comfortable ruling here, and she has gained quite a few followers. Others prefer to avoid conflict, no matter what the expense. Those Fae fear an uprising. They would rather stay here than to have to fight."

"This is all starting to sound a lot like some boring made for TV movie." I groaned. "I never even wanted to be a queen or your *Chosen One*. I just want my normal life back, but I guess that can never happen now."

"Unfortunately, that part of your life is pretty much over, Callie." He said. "It may be for the best if you started to embrace who you are and learn all that you can about our people and our way of life."

Maybe he was right. I could never go back home. There was nothing left for me there. I definitely did not want to go back to Petrona and I had no idea how long Kailen and the people of Drake would let me stay here. Queen Lilith had probably already sent her guards out to search for me. If they found me here, I was sure that there would be trouble.

"Okay, where do I start?" I asked as a pleasantly pudgy woman with curly dark hair brought me a bowl of stew.

"I think the first thing that you need to do is to learn to control your glamour." He explained. "What color are my wings?"

I started to giggle. "Is this some sort of trick? You do not have wings."

"Hmm, that is quite odd. I do indeed have wings, Callie. As do you and I am not using glamour." He said.

This news had me turning around in my seat. "Kailen, I do not have wings. I think that I would know it if I had wings." I strained my neck trying to get a good look at my back.

"It is all a part of the magic, Callie." He explained. "I am afraid that your parents have cast glamour over your eyes as well as your wings. Try this, close your eyes and concentrate. Now envision the glamour dropping away from you, as if it were a curtain. Now open your eyes. Tell me what you see."

"Oh my gosh! Kailen! It is true! Your wings are beautiful!" They were beautiful; they were like the wings of an exotic butterfly. They shimmered in bold shades of green and blue. I looked around and I noticed several more pairs of elaborately decorated wings. My mouth hung open in amazement.

"Callie, look at your wings." Kailen said in awe.

I turned so that I could look toward my back. My wings were glorious. They were a shimmering gold with elaborate designs scrolled in a darker shade from the top to the bottom. I could hardly believe that they were real.

"Can I fly?" I asked, a little breathless.

"Oh yes, you can do anything you want. All that you have to do is think about it." He said with a grin.

I envisioned myself flying across the cavern and landing near the passageway. Before I could say a word I was soaring through the air.

I got a little nervous so I imagined myself landing gently onto my feet, and so I did. "This is amazing!" I yelled as I clapped my hands together and did a little bounce.

After I played a little longer, I sat back down next to Kailen. He went on to tell me the rest of the things that he thought I need to know about being a fairy.

I learned that once we reach adulthood, we barely age. We were nearly immortal, the only thing that could really hurt us was iron. That must have been what the guards used to destroy my parents.

Anger began to boil in my veins whenever I thought about their deaths. I would have to do something to make them proud. To show that their deaths were not in vain. But what? I would have to work on that in the days to come.

Kailen and the other villagers had me practice using my glamour. Once I got the hang of it, I could make my wings disappear and then reappear within seconds. They also showed me how to tuck them against my back so that they would not get in my way when I was not using them. They were a bit cumbersome now that I knew that they were there.

All too soon I noticed that some of the villagers were starting to retire for the night. I felt a little awkward being there. I started to think that maybe I should make my way back into the tunnel. I really did not want to be a burden.

"Callie, you must stay. We have prepared a place for you to sleep for the night. I insist." Kailen said as he directed me toward one of the wooden shacks.

I could not argue. I really had nowhere else to go and the thought of having to sleep in the cold damp tunnel with the bugs and rats was not very appealing. So, reluctantly I followed him and settled in for the night.

7

I slept fairly well in the room that Kailen had made up for me. It was not much. Just a small room in his little wooden shack. There was a sturdy bed and he made sure that I had plenty of blankets and a comfortable pillow. It made me sad to think of Lilith in that huge house with all of those posh bedrooms while Kailen and his friends had to live out here like this.

The people of Drake had a few guys that would sneak into Petrona to get supplies from time to time. They were there when I came. That is why the door was unlocked. Apparently, they had connections in the city and were allowed to come in when they needed to.

I woke pretty early and I could hear shuffling around in the village, probably some of the women preparing the morning meal. Kailen must have still been asleep because his home remained pretty quiet. Except for his soft snore that I could hear drifting from his bedroom.

The main living area of his little shack was sparsely decorated with a few pieces of furniture. There was a small bathroom where I was able to shower. All of the cooking was communal and done outside, so there was no kitchen.

A few trinkets were scattered about on shelves and small handmade tables. They looked like things that he must have collected from the human world. There was a gold pocket watch and a compass proudly display on a shelf on one wall. In addition, another shelf was lined with a collection of books. Mostly classics and do-it-yourself manuals.

There were candles of various sizes and colors scattered about because there was no electricity here in Drake. I lit one of the candles and settled into his small sofa to think. I needed to figure out where I was going to go from here.

I definitely did not want to go back to Petrona and I was afraid of what the queen might do to me if I did. Returning to Louisiana was out of the question. I did not think that I could bear to live there without my family, and I had no idea how I would be able to support myself. I was really in trouble.

I had only sat for a short time before I heard Kailen start to stir in his bedroom. "Good morning Princess, I mean Callie." He said as he entered the living room.

"Good morning." I replied as I smiled at him. "Kailen, how did you know that I was the princess when I first arrived in Drake?" I asked.

"That is an easy question, Callie." He said. "I could tell by your wings."

"My wings? But I thought that you could not see my wings." I said with dismay.

"You could not see your wings Callie, to me they were the most beautiful wings that I had ever seen." He said and I started to blush. "They are even more beautiful than your mother's were, and hers were lovely."

"What did my mother's look like?" I asked wishing that I could have seen them.

"They were silver and trimmed in gold. They were very beautiful. Your father's were steel grey and outlined in black, but I have never seen any that were quite like yours." He explained.

"But everyone here has beautiful wings, how are mine any different?" I asked.

"Yours are true to your bloodline, Callie. Only a true heir has wings of gold or silver." He answered with a smile. "Actually, I have never witnessed anyone with gold wings before. It is quite rare. As are the designs that cover them."

There was no denying who I was now. "Why didn't anyone in Petrona notice my wings then?" I asked.

"Petrona stays shrouded by a powerful glamour spell. The queen wants to pretend that she is human. She feels like they are the superior beings because they live on the surface while we have been driven here." He stated.

I was trying to let all of these things sink in when Kailen finally broached the subject that I had been dreading all morning.

"We need to start preparing a proper house for you today, Callie. Once we get the main structure built, you can come in and decorate it to your liking." He said.

"Kailen," I said hesitantly. "I can't stay here. The queen's guards are probably out searching for me right now. There is no telling what she would do if she found me here. I can't put you or these kind people in jeopardy like that."

"Callie, where else will you go? You have no choice. We will consider you our true queen, and we would proudly protect you until our last breath." He pledged.

"I do not know where I will go, and I am very honored that you would offer such a kind thing. But, I can't accept. I planned to continue through the tunnels until I could find a place of my own, far from the reaches of the queen and her guards." I answered.

"You can't keep running away Callie." He looked at me very seriously. "And you would never last for very long on your own like that. This place is your home, always. Petrona is your home as well. You just have to claim it."

That all sounded good, but I knew that my life would never be that easy. I needed to find some place that I could call my own. Some place that I would have time to learn about the fairy ways without others getting hurt trying to protect me. If I ever did want to be queen, I needed to be prepared to take over a powerful woman like Lilith.

"Kailen, I am only an eighteen year old girl. Last week I was still going to high school. I have only known that fairies existed for a few days. I know nothing of being a fairy princess, let alone a queen. I have only discovered that I had wings just yesterday. I cannot take on Lilith. Not now. There is so much left for me to learn. I have to go. I have to leave today Kailen, before they track me here."

Kailen sat looking down at the floor. He did not say anything for a long time. When he finally looked up at me, he locked his eyes with mine. "Callie, if you must go, if there is no other way, then I am going with you."

"No Kailen. I could never ask you to do that!" I said in alarm. "These people need you here. You can't leave them."

"They will do just fine without me. My brothers are here, and so are many others that are capable of leading them if they need it. I have no other ties to this place and you need help. You could never learn to fight or use your fairy magic on your own. You can't do this by yourself, Callie." He gave me a stern look, and I resigned.

"Fine." I said. "If you truly want to come with me, then I can't stop you. But, you have to know that I have no idea where I am going. I am pretty sure that Lilith's guards will be looking for me and I do not know what they will do to me, or to you if they find me. Brokk has already tracked me in the human world. He should have no trouble tracking me down here."

I found myself absent-mindedly twisting Brokk's ring around my finger.

"Ugh, Brokk." He groaned. "I know the consequences. I know exactly what you are up against. All of the people from Drake came here at some point to escape Lilith's wrath. I also know that it will be different with you. She will want to make sure that you never come back to claim the throne. That is why I can't let you go alone."

Kailen went about the village making arrangements with his brothers and some of the other men and women. In Drake, there were no kings and queens. There was only a village council that was made up of several members of the community. Kailen's departure meant that someone would have to be elected to take his place, but the council felt sure that a suitable person could be found to take his spot.

We spent the rest of the morning gathering supplies. Kailen found two large backpacks that he stuffed with as much food and water as we could carry. Plus blankets and a few changes of clothes. He also brought along a large knife that he strapped to his waist. Once he was certain that we had everything that we may need, we said goodbye to the villagers. We would be leaving during the night, once everyone was settled.

I sat on the bed in Kailen's home while he paced the floors in the living room. We both should have been resting for the long trek ahead of us, but there was a strange tension in the air.

I could not put my finger on it, but obviously, Kailen felt it too.

I stepped into the living room and watched Kailen as he walked in a circle from one end of the small room to the other. He stopped and looked at me when he heard me approach.

"Something is not right." He said. His eyes glowed with nervous anticipation.

"What do you think it is?" I asked softly.

"I am not sure but I think that we should go. Now, before it is too late." He whispered.

I nodded my head and collected my things. We stepped out of the house into the shroud of night. Most of the lanterns had long been extinguished in an attempt to conserve their precious oils. Kailen stayed close behind me as we made our way through the maze of wooden shacks toward the exit.

Kailen froze and pulled me back by my arm as we heard a loud commotion at the entrance to the cavern. We peered into the darkness, searching for some explanation of the sound. Three shadowed figures moved into cavern through the doorway and stood as they glanced around at the village.

"Search every corner! Bring the villagers out and question every one of them! I want to find her fast so that we can get back to the city!" One of the men called.

Before our eyes, an army of the queen's guards poured into the cavern. Each heading off into a different direction. They kicked in doors and forced people out of their homes as they searched each one for a sign of me.

"We have to do something!" I said to Kailen.

"No, we can't Callie." He said. "It would be worse if they actually found you here. The villagers can take care of themselves. This is not the first time that they have encountered the queen's guards. Come on, this way."

He led me behind a row of houses and to the far wall of the cavern. He pointed to a small hole at the base of the wall and said, "Through here."

"We can not go through there!" I argued. "We will never fit."

"We have to, Callie. Crawl through it, I will be right behind you." He urged.

The sound of the guards drawing near was all of the encouragement that I needed. I got down on my knees, took a deep breath, and crawled in through the hole. The rocky walls ripped at my skin as the passage narrowed. The gravel beneath me imbedded painfully into my palms and knees, and I whimpered in pain.

"Just keep going Callie, it's not far now." Kailen called from somewhere behind me.

I pushed on into the total darkness. I felt like the world was closing in and about to swallow me up. I tried hard to control my breathing, taking in long slow breaths as I moved forward.

I had to hold in a scream as something small and furry scampered across my hand. I did not know if I would be able to stand it much longer. I wanted to curl up into a ball and cry. I still could not believe what was happening to me.

The passage turned at a sharp angle and once I was past it, I could sense the air change. I let out a sigh of relief. I knew the end of the tight space was approaching.

I tried to hurry myself along when suddenly the ground beneath me gave way and I tumble out of the wall and landed onto the hard tunnel floor.

8

"Callie!"

I heard my name, and I recognized the voice, but it was not Kailen. I righted myself and leaned my back against the hole, hoping to deter Kailen from spilling out into the trap. I did not notice any sounds coming from inside so I could only assume that he heard it too and waited.

"Brokk?" I asked, as I peered into the tunnel toward the figure now running towards me.

"Callie, you are okay!" He said as he dropped to his knees in front of me. "We have been searching everywhere for you! What are you doing out here?"

"What do you want, Brokk?" I could not hide the ice in my voice.

I began to brush the dirt and gravel from my palms and knees. I was trying to do all that I could to avoid having to look into his eyes. I feared that if I did, our crazy bond thing would cause me to get all loopy and I would end up back in his arms.

"Callie, I am so sorry. Please, let me help you up. We have to get you back to the city." He tried to pull me from the floor by my arm but I jerked it away. He looked at me in confusion.

"Callie, please. I said that I was sorry. Just let me help you get back to the palace, we can talk about everything later. But right now we really need to go." He insisted.

"Hold on a minute Brokk!" I yelled as I jumped to my feet. "There is nothing to talk about and I am not going anywhere with you. You knew what Lilith had planned for me! You knew and you just left me there! You knew that she was going to kill my parents! That is why you went back!"

I could no longer hold back my tears. Seeing Brokk was just more than I could take.

"Okay, I knew that she only wanted to use you for her own benefit, but I also knew that she would never hurt you. I was afraid that she might try to harm your parents, and yes, that is why I went back. Nevertheless, I was too late Callie, and I am so sorry for that. Please, just come with me now and we can fix this." He pleaded.

"Fix this? How can you fix this?" I stammered. "You stole me away from the only home that I ever knew! You brought me to that awful place where I was locked away like some kind of animal! You say that she would never hurt me, but what was she going to do after she was through with me? Do you think that she was really going to let me go?"

"Queen Lilith would never hurt you, Callie." He said as his blue eyes started to get misty.

"You have to know that. I am sorry that you were not happy with your arrangement there, but if we talk to her. If she knew how unhappy you were, I know that she would change things."

"She killed my family! Do you really think that she cares if I am unhappy with my *arrangements*?" I yelled. "And you, you did nothing to stop her! You just let her destroy everything that I have ever loved! You knew what she was going to do and you never said a word!" I had just about all that I could take of this. "There is no talking to her, you know that as well as I do. She brought me here to use me, and when she was through with me, she would have killed me too. Just like she killed my parents."

I sobbed so hard that tremors racked my body. I could barely stand.

"Callie that is enough!" He growled as he moved for me. "Let's go. Now."

He grabbed hold of my arm and started to yank me down the tunnel. I don't know what came over me but I jerked him back. Shock registered on his face as he turned to look at me.

He moved toward me again and this time I did not hesitate. I lifted my leg and kneed him in the groin with all of my might. He crumpled over clutching himself, and I followed up by delivering a massive blow to the left side of his face.

His head flew back with the force of my fist, knocking him off balance. He landed onto the floor with a thud.

I leapt on top of him, straddling his waist. He struggled to sit up but I would not let him. I raised my fist and landed blow after blow to his face.

I could not stop myself. The rage and despair from the events that took place over the last week came boiling out of me with every strike of my hand. I could feel my tears burning my eyes but I ignored them. I wanted nothing more than to hurt Brokk, just as he had hurt me.

I heard my name echoing through the depths of the tunnel, but I never relented. I continued my onslaught of punches until I felt warm hands grab onto my elbow just as I was about to land another blow. I snapped up with eyes blazing to see who was blocking my fury.

I stared at Kailen with hate in my eyes for just a moment. Then the realization of my actions hit me like a ton of bricks and I slumped over against his chest and sobbed. My hand throbbed from the abuse that I had just put it through and it was starting to swell. The skin around some of my knuckles was cracked and bleeding. I clutched it to me to try an ease some of the pain.

Kailen pulled me off of Brokk and rested his back against the tunnel wall as he held me to him. A deep sorrow filled me, and then remorse. My tears soaked his shirt as I cried for my parents, and for the life that I could no longer have. I cried for the pain that was still sharp in my heart from Brokk's betrayal. I cried out of desperation for having no place to go.

I had never felt so lost and alone.

As my tears began to slow, I remembered where I was. I raised my head to see that Kailen was watching me. He still held me cradled in his arms as he wound his hand in my hair and stroked the back of my head. He had been whispering sweet encouragements in my ear, but I had never heard them. I was too lost in my own grief to hear anything.

I looked over my shoulder to see that Brokk was still lying in the middle of the tunnel. His arms were splayed out at an awkward angle and his head was turned to the side, facing me. His left eye was swollen and a dark purple bruise was spreading across his left brow and cheek.

"Is he alive?" I asked Kailen in a quiet tone.

"Yes, he is alive." He said with a chuckle. "But I think he will be out cold for a while. I don't know about you, but I do not want to be around when he wakes up."

"I think you are right." I said as I started to stand.

I wiped the remaining tears from my face, and brushed myself off. Kailen picked up my backpack and helped me put it on, and then pulled on his own.

"We better move fast, I doubt that the rest of the guards are going to be far behind him." He said gesturing to Brokk.

I looked at Brokk for a long moment. It was hard to believe that it had only been a little over a week since I was in the tunnel with him. I remembered how easy trusting him had been, even after all that he had done. I never would have considered myself that naive. There was just something about him that drew me to him, even when my entire being was screaming to me that I should be afraid.

The way he penetrated me with those eyes. Just the thought of them filled me with a deep regret. I thought that I was falling in love with him. I looked at the ring on my finger as it held my swollen hand near my heart. I wished that things could have turned out different, that we could have had a life together. I guess it was just never really meant to be.

I debated on whether or not I should return the ring to Brokk. When he first gave it to me, I had taken it as a promise of a future that would be full of love and wonder. I guess that I had been hoping for a fairytale. I just did not see how that would be possible anymore.

"Callie?" Kailen called softly.

"I'm coming." I answered, and then I walked away. The ring remained on my finger. I made a promise never to take it off, and I intended to keep that promise. At least until Brokk decided that he no longer wanted for me to have it.

"Kailen." I called as we started walking. "Have you ever felt something so strongly for someone that you went against all else because you wanted so badly to believe that it was right?"

"Do you mean Brokk?" He asked indifferently.

I hesitated for a moment and then answered honestly. "Yes."

"You have known Brokk since your birth, Callie." He stated. "I was afraid of this when I first heard you mention that it was he who came for you. When you were young, your mother had a good friend who often visited the palace. Her husband was a prominent figure in Petrona at the time. Your mother believed it would be in the best interest of all if you were to marry their son. Brokk."

"So, that is why he said that I belonged to him." I said.

"You both spent a great deal of time together as children, but after your parents took you away things began to change. Lilith was very jealous of your mother's title. So when she named herself as queen, she cast out all of your mother's followers. Brokk's father was demoted to a lowly guard, and therefore Brokk was too. He became very bitter. I think that is why he has tried so hard to please Lilith, even if it meant hurting you. I think that he hoped that it would gain him access to the title again."

"I can not believe that all that has happened has been because of Lilith's greed and lust for power." I said in disbelief. "But Brokk? I never got that he was bitter or that he was after any title or power. He may have been trying to please her, but I honestly want to believe that he must have had good intentions. He was very worried about the state of the city and the people there."

Kailen scoffed. "You are too kind, Callie. Far more so than he deserves."

"I don't know about that. Especially after what I just did to him." My regret was really beginning to tug at my heart.

"I think that he was just feeling some of the same things that I was feeling. I really don't know how to explain it Kailen, but it was like we were drawn to each other by some unseen force. Like a bond almost. I even feel it now, out here. It is all that I can do to keep myself from running back to him."

He thought about that for a while. "I have never heard of anyone being bonded to another the way that you are describing. I cannot imagine how that could be possible. I don't even think that fairy magic could do something like that."

That was strange. I had considered the idea of fairy magic, but I really did not know enough about it. If Kailen didn't think that it were possible then maybe it was something else entirely. I had to stop thinking about it. I had to try to put as much distance between Brokk and myself as possible.

I did not want to think about being anybody's princess either. This world was definitely corrupt, and Lilith was surely the heart of the problem. However, that did not excuse the fact that I was still just a teenage girl. How was I going to take over a whole kingdom? Let alone run one. And how was I supposed to get around Lilith? I was running from her right now.

What I really needed to focus on was what I was going to do to survive down here. I had no idea where I was going, or what I was going to do when I got there. I was not even sure how long Kailen would be able to stay with me. I knew that he meant well, but he had a life and a family of his own.

I doubted that he would leave me out here alone. Not unless he truly had to, but I also could not ask him to stay. It would save us both a lot of trouble if I could just go back to Petrona, but there is no way that I could. Even if the queen didn't kill me, she would make sure that I never left my room again. That was no way to live either.

9

Kailen hurried down the passage heading away from Petrona and I followed. I don't know which direction that was exactly, there was no way to tell down there. Before we left Drake, Kailen had consulted some of the older villagers who had explored parts of the underground world over the years, so I trusted him to lead. The villagers told him that there were several more caverns along our route and that eventually we would have to cross a large underground river. No one had really explored any farther than there, so once we crossed it, we were on our own.

A few hours into our journey my feet started to ache and I started to moan. I was still wearing Bree's servant dress and matching black ballet slippers. The slippers did not provide much protection for my tender feet against the rocky ground.

I knew that Kailen had some extra clothes packed for me but I didn't want to use them yet because I didn't know how long it would be until I could get more if they were ripped or torn.

"Come on Callie," he encouraged. "You can make it a little farther."

"Why can't we just fly? Isn't that what these huge wings are for?" I whined.

"This passage is not wide enough to fully open our wings, and there are sharp boulders jutting out everywhere. You have only tried to fly a few times, it just would not be safe."

I pouted but I trudged on. The tunnel looked wide enough to me, but I figured he was probably right. I was already pretty bruised up from everything that I had gotten myself into over the past few days. I did not need to add a concussion or broken limb to the list of things that were wrong with me.

"Look Callie!" I looked up to see that Kailen was pointing to something up ahead on the floor of the tunnel. He ran ahead of me to investigate. I watched as he picked up some kind of rag or cloth and turn it over in his hands.

"This is not good." He was shaking his head.

"What is it?" I asked as I hurried to catch up.

"It is an insignia. It is from one of the guards uniforms. They must have already come through here. I just hope that they have already made their way back." He looked very grim when he said that.

I started getting worried that we would get caught. I never imagined that the guards would have made it this far ahead of us. The party that ransacked the city must have not been the only guards out looking for me. This was the last thing that we needed. I certainly did not feel up to having to fight anyone else.

I looked down at my hands to find that my knuckles were still swollen and sore from the fight that I had with Brokk. Well, it was not much of a fight really. It was more like me, kicking his ass. Regardless, I was too exhausted to take on much more in one day.

"Maybe we should start looking for someplace that we can hide out and get some rest." I said to Kailen. "If they do come back through here and we are out in the tunnel they will definitely catch us."

"That is true," he said thoughtfully. He started looking around for a good spot as we continued to walk. Several moments later, he stopped in the middle of the tunnel and stared up toward the top of the tall rocky wall.

"Do you think that we could make up to there?" He pointed to a crevice that was at least four feet above our heads. "We only need to be able to climb in and lie down. There should be just enough space in there for that."

I didn't see what it would hurt to check it out and I was definitely ready to take a break. I had to give him a boost to where he could pull himself the rest of the way up onto the ledge. Once he checked things out, he leaned back out.

"This is a pretty tight squeeze, but it should do for the night. Here, let me pull you up."

He reached down for me and hoisted me up onto the ledge with ease.

I had to crouch down in the shallow space to keep from hitting my head on the ceiling as I turned to stretch my legs out over the blankets that Kailen had already spread out as a make shift bed.

The crevice was only about five feet wide and about three feet tall, so it was pretty close quarters. Especially since, it also had to accommodate our backpacks.

I picked up the remaining blanket and fought to spread it out over the both of us. Kailen grabbed one side and pulled it over him to help me get it straight.

"Sorry." I said, feeling a little bashful all of the sudden. "I hope that you don't mind sharing."

"I don't mind." He said with a reassuring smile.

We laid there in the crevice chest to chest, just looking off into space for a long time without saying anything. It was the first time that I had felt truly relaxed in a very long time.

Although we were trying to avoid the royal guard, and we were searching for a place to make a new start, I wasn't afraid. Yes, my future was looking pretty uncertain at this point, but that really didn't bother me. Right there in that hole high above the rest of the world, the underworld anyway, I finally felt like everything was going to be okay.

"Callie?" Kailen said in whispering, pulling me from my thoughts.

"Yeah?" I asked.

"Do you remember anything about the time you spent in Petrona when you were young?" He asked.

"No, all of my memories are from my time on the surface. At least I think they are. I remember taking ballet lessons, and my first day of school. All of those things happened around my home in Louisiana. Why do you ask?"

"It is just that I remember you, from before you left. You were very young, maybe five or six years old. I took you by the hand and walked with you to the depot on the surface where a driver was to pick up you and your family and take you to your new life."

I closed my eyes and tried hard to remember anything from that time. It struck me as odd that all of these guys remembered me from when I was young but I had no recollection of them.

"I was eight years old. I just remember how you were so scared, you did not want to leave your home here. I gave you a coin and told you to always keep it close to you. That way you would always know that I was with you in your heart and you would never have to feel alone."

I could not answer. I could not find the words. My body started to tremble involuntarily. How could this be? I thought to myself.

"Callie?" He said. I could hear the fear in his voice.

I opened my eyes and stared into his as they searched my face for an understanding of my sudden change in mood.

"Callie? Is something wrong?" He asked again.

I could not seem to find my voice. Without pulling my eyes from his, I reached into my shirt and pulled out a long gold chain. On the end of it dangled an ancient gold coin. It had a crescent moon with a god's face stamped on one side, and a horse over a rising sun on the other.

He pulled his eyes from mine and watched the coin spinning as it dangled from my fingertips. He reached out, caught it in his hand, and twisted the chain gently around his fingers, and then he cupped my hand in his. He pulled me toward him gently, and softly touched his lips to mine.

I held my eyes closed as I savored the gentle warmth that was spreading from my lips throughout the rest of my body.

I felt that if I opened my eyes at that very moment, I would be glowing.

He pulled away from me all too quickly as we heard a sudden clambering on the tunnel floor below us.

"The queen is not going to be happy." A voice drifted up.

"We have searched every inch of this tunnel. There is no sign of her. She probably fell into the water as she tried to cross the river and washed away." Another answered.

"Perhaps you are right. I doubt that she could have made it past there. I just hope that is good enough for the queen."

I froze wide-eyed as I stared at Kailen. He held one finger to his lips to remind me to keep quiet. There was a brief moment of the sound of shuffling feet, and then all was quiet again.

"Do you think that they are gone?" I whispered.

"It sounds as if they are, but we should try to keep still and as quiet as possible just to be sure." He answered.

I peered out into the darkness, nearly holding my breath, but no more sounds came from the tunnel. I looked back to Kailen to find him watching me intently. I allowed myself to relax a little and gave him a soft smile.

He reached for me again and pulled me to him. I turned so that my back was pressed against his chest. I could feel his warm breath on my neck as he buried his face in my hair. I had just had my first kiss. I was not sure how I felt about that. I didn't know what it could have meant. Kailen had never shown any interest in me romantically until that moment, but now I was nestled in his arms.

My mind kept going back to Brokk lying in the tunnel. I should not have lost my temper like that, he did not deserve it. Once again, the tears started to slide down my face. I didn't think that I had ever cried so much in my whole life as I had in the last few weeks.

I had not known either of them for very long, but already I found myself lost in confusion. I truly believed that Brokk cared for me, and I was feeling almost ashamed that I was here with Kailen but Brokk kind of fed me to the wolves. He handed me over to Lilith without a thought. At least that is what it felt like to me.

Kailen has done nothing but try to help me from the minute that he met me. I had thought of him more as a brother or a teacher than a potential boyfriend, but I let him kiss me. I didn't even try to resist. Actually, I kind of liked it.

"Callie," he whispered softly in my ear pulling me from my thoughts. "Tell me about the necklace."

I rolled slightly so that I could look at him, but not enough that I would break his embrace. I closed my eyes and tried to picture that day.

"I remember being scared." I started. "My parents were very nervous. We were going on a trip and I could not understand their anxiety."

"I remember seeing the sunlight. I remember how the warm rays touched my face as I looked up into the sky." I sat for a moment trying to picture that day. "I remember you pressing the coin into my hand. I remember your smile and your reassurance as I was loaded into a car. I remember watching you standing on the street as the car pulled away."

"You had red hair." I said with a grin.

"Yes." He said with a nod and slight smile.

"I held this coin in my hand throughout our entire journey." I said. "My mother tried to get me to put it away once we had made it to our new home. But I only held it tighter. I told her that I could never let it go, so she had it made into a necklace. I have rarely taken it off since."

He kissed me gently on my forehead, and then he moved to my lips. His tender kisses sent waves of emotion like I have never felt rocking through my body. Brokk may have been who I was supposed to be with, according to what I've heard anyway, but I was beginning to think that I could definitely get used to Kailen. It may not be so bad living as an outcast after all.

We both finally managed to fall asleep at some point during the night. It was the most peaceful sleep that I could ever remember, wrapped there in his arms.

10

I woke to the feel of Kailen softly tracing his finger along my cheek. I smiled before I ever bothered to open my eyes. I wanted to stay here like that forever.

I opened my eyes and he smiled back at me. "Good morning," he whispered softly.

"Hey." I said. "Have you been awake for long?"

"Just for a little while. I did not want to disturb you. You looked so peaceful. I know that you have been through a lot in the past few days. It was nice to see you with your guard down."

I just smiled sheepishly

"We better get moving. We have a lot of ground to cover today." He whispered encouragingly.

I groaned. "Do we have to?"

He nodded. "I wish that we didn't, but hopefully we will find a more permanent place soon."

We set about packing up our little camp the best that we could in the confined space. Kailen lowered himself to the tunnel floor while I changed into a pair faded blues jeans and an old grey t-shirt that was worn just enough to be soft and comfy.

I hurriedly tried to rake a comb through my tangled hair, but soon gave up and tied it into a messy ponytail.

"Toss me the bags when you are ready, then I will help you climb down." Kailen called from below.

"Okay, I am ready." I tossed him the packs, and then I laid on my stomach as I swung my legs down from the ledge. I was dangling by my arms when I felt Kailen grab hold of my legs. He gently lowered me to the ground.

"Thanks." I said as I brushed myself off.

We hefted our packs onto our backs and headed further into the depths of the tunnel.

Kailen's hand somehow managed to find mine and he held onto it, helping me over rocks and debris for the rest of the day.

It was nice. I have never had a boyfriend, but I hoped that it would be something like that. I can't say for sure, but it just felt right.

I know that I felt something for Brokk, very briefly of course, when I was with him. Maybe it was a familiarity from some forgotten time, or maybe it was fear. It could have just been that he was the first guy to treat me like a desirable woman. However, the short time that I spent with Brokk seemed nothing like the feeling that was blooming inside of me for Kailen.

I smiled to myself as I remembered that tender first kiss. I could hardly imagine how much my life has changed in such a short amount of time. Ten days ago, I was an awkward high school senior that never even had a date. Today I was a fairy princess, holding hands with a gorgeous guy.

I also went from a happy home to being homeless and traipsing around what was basically a sewer. And I really missed my parents. I could not believe that they were really gone.

Kailen must have noticed my sudden gloom, because he tugged me closer to him and put his arm around my shoulders, hugging me tightly.

"You okay?" He sounded concerned.

"I think I am just a little homesick. I will be okay."

At least I hoped that I would be okay. My world was changing faster than I could keep up with, and not even in a good way. I could only hope that things could not possibly get any worse for me than they were right then.

He looked at me for few moments more, then brushed a stray piece of hair back from my face and tucked it behind my ear.

"Things are going to get better, Callie. You will see. Soon we will transform you into an amazing warrior who will instill fear into anyone who dares to cross you. You will take back what is yours and then you will live happily ever after with the guy of your dreams. Just how a Fairy Tale should be."

I could not help but to let out a giggle at that. "What if I don't want that? Not the part about the guy and the happily ever after. But what if I don't want to go back to Petrona? What if I don't want to be a queen?"

"Callie, you can not hide out forever." He shook his head as if he started to say something else but thought better of it. "Let's just take one day at a time. We can worry about all of that later."

"Okay, you are probably right. One day at a time."

The one thing that he was definitely right about is that I couldn't hide forever. I had to get out of the tunnels and try to have some semblance of a life. I just did not want to think about having to go back to the city and deal with Lilith. Or Brokk. There had to be another way.

We had walked for at least another hour when we finally started to hear a steady loud roar. Kailen looked at me and then we both turned and started to run towards the sound. It grew louder and louder as we approached. It was nearly deafening.

There just ahead of us was an enormous river right through the center of the earth. The water flowed rapidly past us with tremendous force. It was at least thirty feet wide and there was no way that I could imagine that we would ever be able to get across it.

"We need to find a way around!" Kailen yelled over the noise. "There has to be a way!"

He backed up and started to look around. There appeared to be nothing but the shear rock walls of the tunnel.

"Hello!" We barely heard calling across the rumble of the river.

We stopped and looked at each other for a moment, and then we heard it again. "Hello!"

Far on the other side of the river, I noticed a man standing on the ledge waving his arms frantically over his head.

"Look over there, Kailen." I said pointing.

"You have to climb to where the river narrows!" The man yelled while pointing downstream.

Kailen leaned around the wall to look in the direction that the man was pointing.

"The river narrows a good ways down. It looks like we may be able to cross there, but we have to climb along the ledge to get there."

I peered around Kailen at the narrow ledge that jutted out from the wall along the river's edge. It was only about six to ten inches wide and then it dropped off. The river was at least ten feet down.

"No way!" I shook my head. "There has to be another way."

"It's the only way that I can see to get across. The river is much too fast to try to cross here. You can do it Callie." He encouraged. "I will be right behind you if anything should happen."

I watched him for a minute. "Okay, I trust you."

I trusted Kailen, but I did not trust myself. I could be a bit clumsy sometimes and I had never done anything like that before. The closest that I had been to something like that was hopping across the streams in the mountains when I went on vacation with my parents.

Kailen helped me around the wall and out onto the ledge. I tried to keep a hold on the rocks that jutted out from the wall as I slid my feet little by little toward a small bank that was at least fifty yards away.

Once I was a few feet down, Kailen followed me onto the ledge and eased his way along beside me. He repeated little phrases of encouragement the whole while.

Halfway between the tunnel and the narrow riverbank I landed my foot on a small accumulation of rocks. My foot slipped out from under me and sent rocks spilling into the rushing water below. I let out a short scream and clung to the wall as I tried to regain my balance.

"Hang on, Callie." Kailen said as he reached for me.

I tried to hang on but I felt myself losing my grip on the rocks and the next thing that I knew I was falling.

I landed on my back into the frigid water and sunk several feet under. I waved my arms frantically trying to pull myself to the surface.

The strong current propelled me along underneath the water as I struggled to hold my breath for as long as I could.

I could not believe that this was happening to me. After all, that I had been through, how I could I die now? Like this, under the water cold and alone?

I was nearly about to give in to my bodies need to gasp for air when I felt something grip my waist and tug me up and out of the water.

I opened my eyes as I coughed and sputtered, trying to pull as much air into my lungs as I could.

"You are going to be okay." I heard.

That is the last thing that I remember. A sleepy darkened fog settled over my mind and I could no longer hold my eyes open. Slumber overcame me.

When I woke, I found myself lying on the damp rocky ground. I could still hear the deadly roar of the river very close by. My teeth chatter and I had goose bumps all along my arms. My clothes were wet and clinging to my skin.

Then I remembered my fall. I opened my eyes to see that my head was cradled in Kailen's lap and that he was speaking to someone just outside of my vision.

I tried to rise up to see what was going on, but Kailen pushed me back down. He told me to rest as he stroked my hair back from my face.

"I'm okay." I tried again to rise up. "Just really cold. What happened?"

"You fell into the water, and the current carried you away from me before I could get to you. I thought that I had lost you." Kailen said with tears in his eyes. "I am so sorry, Callie." He pulled me up slightly and hung his head so that cheek was resting against my neck.

"It's okay Kailen." I said as I reached up and wound my fingers through his hair, pulling him even closer to me.

I sat there in his lap, breathing him in for a long time. He finally released his grip and pulled away.

"How did I get out?" My voice was hoarse and my throat felt raw.

"Tucker used a long stick to help him reach you and he pulled you out." He gestured to someone sitting a few feet away from us.

I managed to push myself up on my hands enough to see a young sandy haired boy staring intently at me. He was wearing baggy khaki colored pants that were rolled up at the ankles exposing his bare feet. He wore a long sleeve tatter green shirt that I noticed matched the color up his eyes as he blew his hair from his face.

"I'm Tucker Reed, but you can call me Tuck." He held his hand out to me.

"I'm Callie. Thanks for saving me."

"You're lucky that I got to you in time, there is a waterfall just over there." He pointed. "You probably would not have survived the fall if you had gone over it."

I shuttered as I looked in the direction that he pointed.

"What are you doing out here, Tuck?"

"I have lived out here for a while. Ever since my parents died during a battle with the Petrona guards, two years ago."

"I am so sorry." I wondered what might have caused the battle, but I didn't want to pry. I had just met the guy and I wasn't sure how he would react to my asking.

He seemed so young to have been out on his own for so long. "How old are you, Tuck?"

"I am sixteen, but don't worry. I can handle myself pretty well." He swelled his chest up as if to convince me.

"I can see that." I said and smiled.

All of my clothes were wet because I was still wearing my backpack when I fell into the water. Tuck built a small fire on the rocky beach and I laid them out to dry. I slipped into one of Kailen's long shirts and washed the clothes that I had been wearing out in the river and set them to dry as well.

Kailen wrapped one of the blankets from his pack around me and we sat by the fire while Tuck ran down to where the river pooled and tried his luck at catching us some fish for dinner.

"We should ask him to come with us." Kailen said into my ear as I leaned back against his chest.

"Maybe. I could not imagine being on my own like that at his age." I was having a hard enough time dealing with my own parent's death. I could not imagine being fourteen and having to learn to fend for yourself on top of it. At least I had help.

"He seems to be pretty good at surviving out here. I think that he would be good for us to have around and we would be good for him too."

Tuck came back carrying several long silver fish by a string. He removed the scales near the water, and then arranged them on the fire to cook. The roasted fish smelled heavenly. I had not eaten anything other than jerky and cheese crackers for days.

"Tuck?" I asked gently. "I know that we do not really know where we are going, but I thought maybe you would like to come with us. I am learning how hard it is to be out here on your own, and I think that you would be a big help to us. We were hoping to find somewhere that we could set up as a permanent home for a while."

I didn't want to seem like I was mothering him, so I tried to appeal to the survivor side of his ego.

He looked deep in thought for a moment, then shrugged his shoulders and answered. "Sure, I don't really have any reason to stick around here."

So it was settled. Tuck would join us.

We filled ourselves with fresh roasted fish, it had me thinking about my dad. I remembered the times that we would all go camping and how I felt when I had caught a fish for the first time.

I wished that he could have been there with me. He would know what I should do with my life, but I bet he wouldn't appreciate all of my new suitors. I think he was quite relieved that had made it most of the way through school without him having to worry about who I was dating.

Then again, he may very well be glad that I have someone around to help me get through this. I smiled to myself as I thought about that. He would have hated knowing that I was out here alone.

Once I found that my clothes were pretty dry, I slipped back into my jeans and t-shirt, but I regretted having to give Kailen's back to him. It smelled of the spring and the rain, just like him. I wanted to savor that smell.

"Let's get going." Tuck was starting to gather his things as well. "If we can make it there, I know a good place that we can camp for the night."

"Ok then, let's go."

11

Tuck helped us gather up our things and then he led us down the rocky river bed toward the waterfall.

"Where are you going?" I called to Tuck.

"There is a good place to sleep through here. I found it a while back when I first came out here." Tuck said.

Kailen looked a little nervous. "Maybe we should just follow the tunnel. I am not really sure about this."

Tuck stopped walking and turned around to face us.

"The guards patrol the tunnels too much. If you want to avoid them, it is better if we stay where they won't see us." He said.

Kailen hesitated for a moment, but then nodded and started to walk.

Tuck led us down to where the river dropped over the edge of a cliff. It was hard to tell in the dark, but it must have been at least a twenty foot drop.

He turned to the right and I noticed that the wall gave way slightly to reveal a narrow path that tilted down toward the bottom of the ravine.

"You will have to really watch your step. Nobody really comes through here so the path can be pretty dangerous. Try to watch your footing and go slow." Tuck said as he started to descend.

I stepped onto the rocky path and Kailen followed close behind me. It was very steep in some areas and loose gravel caused me to slide several times. Each time I slipped, I dropped down onto my butt to keep from going over the edge. By the time that we made it to the bottom the seat of my jeans were covered in mud and muck.

We stood on the flat ground at the bottom of the cliff to regain our bearings.

"Where to now?" Kailen asked Tuck.

"This way." Tuck answered as he headed back towards the river.

"What's over there?" Kailen asked getting irritated.

Tuck let out a huff and turned back around. "I am just trying to help you out. If you don't trust me you do not have to come, but there is a good place through here."

"Let's just go and check it out." I said trying to ease Kailen's nerves. "We don't know what we are going to find following the tunnel anymore than we do going this way. Tuck has lived down here for a long time. It would not hurt us to trust him."

Kailen gave me a long hard stare and I return the stare with just as much fervor.

"Alright." He let his shoulders relax. "We really don't have anything to lose."

Tuck turned back around and continued walking. I followed close behind and after a few minutes I looked back to see that Kailen followed too.

We made our way back to the waterfall. I stood and watched the powerful flow of water as it cascaded down the side of the cliff. It caused the water to churn violently at the base and large clouds of foam formed all around it.

"Through here." Tuck called over the loud roar of the fall.

I watched as he headed close to the wall and seemed to disappear into the falling water.

"Tuck!" I called frantically.

Tuck leaned back out and motioned for us to follow.

As I approached, I realized that Tuck was standing on a ledge just behind the wall of water. I followed him through it as I felt a soft cold spray of water settle over me.

He ducked into a narrow passage just a few feet from where I was standing and I followed. It was much narrower than the main tunnel that I was used to, and it seemed to weave back and forth, as we made our way through it.

After walking for what seemed to me like forever, but was probably only about fifteen minutes, a funny thing happened. I started to see sunlight up ahead in the distance.

"What is that?" I asked mostly to myself.

"You'll see." Tuck answered.

Kailen grabbed my hand as we headed in the direction of the light. My mouth fell open as the passage ended and we found ourselves standing in a huge cavern. It was almost large enough to fit three Petronas inside of it. Okay, maybe not that big, but still pretty big. It had a tall domed ceiling, and in various spots, there were rays of light shining through illuminating the whole cavern.

Kailen squeezed my hand, and I peered up to find him smiling as he held his other hand to his face to block some of the glare.

"This place is amazing!" I exclaimed.

"I thought you would like it." Tuck said with pride.

"How did you ever find it?" I asked.

"I found the passage behind the waterfall one day when I was out there fishing. I thought it was pretty cool, so I followed it. Then I found this." A huge grin stretched across his face.

"I still come here sometimes when I get tired of the tunnels." He continued. "But it always seemed like too big of a space for just me."

I smiled up at him, but I could hardly process what all of this meant. This could really be my new home. I have no idea how we were going to make it all come together, but it was going to be an amazing.

"Let's find a good spot to set up our things." Kailen said as he started to circle the cavern. "We need somewhere to sleep, somewhere to cook and somewhere to train."

"Train? Train for what?" I looked at him puzzled.

"You have to learn everything there is about being a Fae. That includes being able to fight. You saw some of things that you can encounter here. I may not always be there to protect you. You need to be able to defend yourself."

"I can defend myself." My voice sounded more confident than I felt. However, Kailen wasn't buying it.

"You need to be prepared for anything. Plus, if you are ever planning to take on the queen and her army, you better be ready" He was getting that serious tone to his voice again.

I looked to the ground. I wasn't even sure that I wanted to take on Lilith. I was hoping to just start over new and forget about all of that. I had already been through so much, did I really want to start a war?

Kailen noticed my reservation, but he chose to ignore it. Instead, he walked away and began to set up a place for everyone to sleep for the night. He spread the blankets out in three separate rows close to one wall. Then very neatly, he stacked our clothes and supplies a little further away.

Tuck went back out to the waterfall to try to catch us some dinner. I watched Kailen for a while, he was stacking stones in the center of the cavern forming a pit that we could use to cook.

He was bent over with his back to me and I could not help but notice how good he looked from this angle in his dark blue jeans. I smiled to myself and decided that I should take advantage of our time alone while I still could.

I walked up to him and gently traced my hand down his back and across his tight butt and let it rest just before the top of his leg. He froze for a moment and then stood up slowly to face me.

A little glint of light sparkled in his eyes, and he grabbed me by my waist and pulled me to him. He grinned down at me for just a moment and then pulled me into an embrace. His lips hovered briefly in front of mine and then he pulled away.

My confusion must have been written all over my face, because he just apologized. He said that he was sorry but that was it. He promptly went back to stacking the stones.

I grabbed his arm and turned him back to me. "Kailen, what's going on?"

"You are an incredible lady." He said and he wrapped his arms around me and held me close. "I don't ever want to let you go."

"Then don't." I whispered and leaned into him.

He smiled slightly, but the smile never reached his sorrowful eyes.

"What? Is something wrong?" I asked as I pulled back to look him in his eyes.

He stared at me for a second. "Someday you are going to the queen. I'm just a glorified vagrant. I could never be a part of that world. I should not have kissed you. It wasn't right."

Pain shot through me, my eyes wanted to fill up with tears. "I never even wanted to be queen!" I yelled, and the memory of my first kiss flooded my senses. How could he say that it was a mistake? "I still don't know if I want it! Especially if it means that I can't be with you."

"Callie, you are the queen. Whether you like it or not, that's what you were born to do. Look at you. Look at your wings."

He pointed at my wings as they slowly unfolded themselves from my back.

"I am just a cast off, I have no place in Petrona. They would never accept me there, and I am afraid that it would only hurt your status among the people if I were to allow this to continue."

"Then I won't do it." I crossed my arms in defiance. "They have managed this long without me. Lilith can keep it, I would much rather be here with you."

He pulled me back to him and I wrapped my arms around his waist and held onto him as I never wanted to let go. "We'll figure something out." He said, but he didn't sound very confident.

Tuck came back carrying more of those long silvery fish, and an armload of smooth glossy wood. I pulled away from Kailen and turned to face him.

"I have dinner!" He called as he held up the fish.

"Where did you find all of that wood?" I asked.

"The river carries it here and deposits it along the bank in some of the narrower spots. There is plenty more where this came from, we should stock up."

"Tomorrow you and I can go together and try to bring as much back as we can." Kailen said, straightening himself.

The two of them went about preparing the fish and I went and sat on one of the blankets and leaned against the wall.

Why did Kailen have to keep insisting on me taking over and being queen? I was content to stay right here and just be a normal girl. Well, as normal as I could be under the circumstances.

Maybe he didn't really like me as much as I had hoped. Maybe this was his way of pushing me away. My emotions were starting to get the best of me and I was full of doubt and self-pity.

I had always thought my first kiss would have been with somebody that really loved me. Now I was beginning to regret that I had let him do it. Why did men have to be so complicated?

Tuck brought me a few pieces of the fish once it was cooked, but I didn't really feel like eating. I just felt really drained. I looked at the three separate sleeping areas. The realization of what that meant hit me hard. He didn't even want to be close to me, or sleep near me.

I felt sure that after the night that we spent in the hole over the tunnel he would be holding me like that every night. I guess that I misjudged him. Maybe that night was just a fluke.

I pushed myself down from the wall and lay on my side. Night was beginning to set in and the only remaining light was the soft glow of the fire. I was grateful for that, because I definitely didn't want either of them to see my tears. I couldn't hold them back any longer.

I had never felt as alone as I had since I was brought to this horrible place. My parents were gone, the people from Petrona were evil. Tuck was just a kid and Kailen had pushed me away. Could things possibly suck anymore than right now? I certainly hoped not.

The only thing left for me to do was to fight for what I wanted, I resigned. I just wasn't sure what that was exactly.

If my parents loved me enough to take me away and protect me the way that they did so that I could be queen someday, then maybe that was what I would have to do.

I hated the idea of it though. Not just the fighting, but I hated the idea of being a queen. I just wanted a normal life.

I wanted to date a cute guy, and maybe even get married. I wanted to go to college and teach Literature or History someday. Now all of those dreams were gone in an instant.

I started hating Brokk more and more for taking me from my home. It just wasn't fair. Nobody had ever even told me that this world existed. I was never given a choice in the matter. They could have at least given me a heads up and let me prepare for it.

Prepared on not I was here. I was stuck in a world that I never even knew existed, and I had lost everything that I had ever loved because of it. I could not just sit here and let one evil person destroy everything about my life and do nothing to stop her.

I made up my mind. I would learn all of the ins and outs of being a fairy, and I would get Tuck to teach me to fight like a warrior. I would go to Petrona and take my place. I would do it for my mother.

I might spend the rest of my life alone, but I would honor my mother and the choices that she made for me when she was queen.

Once I had made up my mind, I started getting excited. I could no longer lay there, sleep was far from my mind. I got up and sat close to the fire pit, the fire had gone out but the stones still put out a cozy warmth. I spent the rest of the night trying to figure out all that I needed to do to get myself in shape. It may take me a while, but I was willing to work hard to get what I wanted.

12

The next day I woke up early and found that I was still curled up on the cold stone next to the fire pit. I jumped up and quickly rummaged through my small stack of clothes until I found something suitable to wear for the day. I pulled on a pair of silky grey sweats and a loose fitting white t-shirt. I didn't really have any good shoes so I stayed barefoot. It wasn't so bad anymore, my feet were starting to toughen up after all that I had put them through.

Tuck and Kailen were nowhere in sight so I assumed that they were already out gathering what driftwood they could find along the river.

I moved to the center of the cave, it was a great open area and the ceiling was pretty high. It would be perfect for what I wanted to do. Slowly I began to stretch and prepare myself for the day.

I practiced controlling my wings, which had pretty much stayed flattened against my back since we left Drake.

I found that they responded pretty much like any other body part. I stretched them and fluttered them a few times until I was comfortable with them.

I started practicing being able to start and stop, just as Kailen had briefly explained when I first discovered that I had wings.

I took off quickly as I envisioned myself on the other side of the room. Panic set in for brief moment so I hurriedly envisioned myself landing. I fell to ground with a thud, twisting my ankle. I cried out in pain, but I pulled myself together and got back up.

My ankle throbbed and I bent to rub it. I needed to learn to start and stop more slowly or I would really hurt myself. I had to try again.

This time I pictured myself moving a little slower and more gracefully. I went soaring through the air. The gentle wind that moved over my wings felt amazing. I set myself back down more carefully, then sat down smiling.

I remembered being a little girl out in the bayou with my dad. We were bundled up from head to toe in green camouflage.

I remember watching in awe as a large flock of wood ducks soared overhead and landed on the water without so much as a splash.

This is what it must have felt like to the ducks. Only I think they were a little more graceful.

I stood and took off again, this time I circled the entire cavern. I looked around at the rocky walls and I was amazed to see bird nests and intricate spider webs formed along the outcroppings of rock.

I flew up to the cracked ceiling and hovered close to one of the openings that allowed the sunlight to pour in. A cool breeze carried fresh salty air over me. We must be close to the ocean.

I breathed in deeply and smiled to myself.

I hadn't even noticed Kailen and Tuck entering the cave, until I heard Tuck.

"Oh my god, look at that."

I suddenly lost my concentration and started falling towards them. I didn't even have to scream.

"Land Callie!" Kailen yelled up at me.

But it was too late, I rammed into them at full speed sending them crashing onto the floor with me on top of them. I was definitely going to suffer for this tomorrow. I was lucky I didn't break anything.

I untangled myself from them and quickly folded my wings back away. I tried to help Kailen up but he just shrugged away from me.

"What are you trying to do?" He yelled as he struggled to get to his feet. Wood was scattered all around them.

"I was trying to fly." I said defensively. Who did he think he was yelling at me like that?

"Why didn't you wait for me to help you?" His tone was definitely angry.

"I-I just wanted to see if I could do it." I stammered but I quickly composed myself. "And I don't recall you making any effort." This time I was more fierce and I crossed my arms across my chest.

He let out a growl and turned to start picking up the driftwood. "You should have waited for me."

I turned my back to him and walked away.

I had to fight hard to keep from grimacing at the pain shooting through my ankle. I definitely didn't want anybody to find out that I had injured myself. He would never let me hear the end of that.

Tuck didn't say anything more, he just followed Kailen over to the makeshift fire pit and began to stack the wood.

Nobody spoke to me or even bothered looked at me for a long time. I felt that old familiar pain in my heart. I don't know why it always had to hurt so much when Kailen tried to push me away. I had to get over that. I needed to get away for a while.

While they were busy concentrating on the wood and the fire, I slipped out of the cavern and into the tunnel. I knew that I shouldn't be wondering around out there alone, but they didn't seem to have a problem with leaving me alone today. They didn't even tell me that they were leaving.

I stomped toward the waterfall getting angrier by the minute, but my throbbing ankle reminded me to slow down. I reached the fall and stared at the water for a long time. The tremendous sound of the crashing water helped me to think more clearly. It blocked everything else out.

I had made up my mind the night before to do everything that I could to live up to what my family wanted for me. That included becoming a queen, even though I still didn't know what that meant exactly.

I was lost in my thoughts when I heard a loud noise echo behind me. Even over the sound of the falls. It sounded like rocks falling and hitting the rocky floor, but I couldn't be sure. It was probably Kailen or Tuck coming to make sure that I wasn't doing anything stupid.

I decided not to turn around. I just wanted to be left alone, and I didn't want to give Kailen the satisfaction of thinking that he had gotten to me. I stood at the riverbank listening to see how close they were when I suddenly felt a hand clamp down over my mouth and I was violently jerked backward.

My eyes must have been as big as saucers, as I struggled to break the hold that he had on me. He pulled me backward toward the path that led to the top of the falls. I cried out but my screams were muddled by his grip on my mouth.

"A pretty girl like you shouldn't be wandering around these dark tunnels by yourself" A strange voice said in my ear.

Fear suddenly ripped through me. No, this was definitely not Kailen or Tuck. I began fight against him with all that I had in me, but it was no use. I hated feeling this powerless.

"What have you got there, Sty" I heard another voice call from above.

"I found us a little treat." Sty called back with a sinister laugh.

He yanked me up the path, and his friend met him part of the way and helped him pull me to the top. Their stench filled my nose and I wanted to gag. It had obviously been some time since they had bathed and now I knew why he was called Sty.

On the top of the cliff, I was able to get a good look at the buddy. He was tall and wiry thin. His greasy hair was matted around his filthy face. He smiled at me with teeth that were black and broken as he eyed me up and down.

"Nice catch old boy." He said as he patted Sty on the back. "Bring her in here."

Sty drug me away from the ledge and threw me hard against the wall.

"Somebody help me!" I screamed as the two of them stood in front of me gawking.

"Scream all you want, nobody can hear you over the sound of the water." Sty said with a grin.

Sty was just as grimy as his friend. He was a good bit shorter, but he had the same slick dark hair and toothless grin. His breath was vile and I had to cough to keep myself from vomiting.

"What do you want?" I said in disgust. They just kept grinning. those gruesome toothless grins.

Sty grabbed me by my arms and pulled me to my feet. "I just want a little kiss sweet thing. It's been a long time since I had a girl as pretty as you."

He moved in with that mouth and I kicked him hard in the shin. He reached down for it and I was about to make an escape but his friend caught me by my hair and yanked me back.

"Now where do you think you're going?" He held me up by my hair and pain ripped across my scalp and my toes barely grazed the floor. "You're going to be a feisty one I see. All the better."

He dropped me back onto my feet but he did not release my hair. Sty came back over and slapped me hard across the face. The blow had my head swimming and I could taste fresh blood in my mouth.

He just kept laughing that stupid laugh. "I bet you won't try that again."

I spat at him, and he hit me again. The pain was almost overwhelming and I nearly passed out. I needed to do something to get away from these guys, I just wasn't sure what.

"Hey!" I wasn't sure where it came from but I was relieved to hear it.

Sty and his buddy jerked around to see what was going on. The problem is that tall and skinny never let go of my hair. I felt sure that if he didn't let go soon, I was going to have a major bald spot.

"What do you want?" Sty yelled back.

"Just drop the girl and step away."

I struggled to turn so that I could see who was approaching, but as soon as I realized that it was Tuck my face fell.

He was too young to fight these guys alone. He was definitely going to get hurt or worse, and it would be all my fault if he did. I should never have stormed out like that.

"Boy, just get on out of here before you get yourself in trouble." Sty called to him as he took on a defiant stance.

Tuck never faltered. He did not stop until he was a few feet in front of us.

He watched the two slime balls for a minute and then he calmly lifted his arm back and pulled out a thick shiny sword. It curved in the middle and the handle was inlaid with gold.

"I'm only going to ask you one more time." Tuck stepped forward again.

"Drop the girl."

Relief filled my body as the guy finally released me. My head still ached and so did my ankle as I plopped back down onto it, but I was free. I crawled to where I could position myself behind Tuck and regroup.

"Now, get out of here!" Tuck yelled still holding up the blade as if he were about to strike. "If I ever see you around here again, that will be the last time!"

"Let's get out of here, Sully!"

So that was tall and ugly's name.

The two of them took off running back down into the darkness of the tunnel.

"Are you okay?" Tuck held out a hand to help me up.

I got to my feet, rubbing the back of my head. "Yeah, I think so."

"What were you doing out here by yourself?" He didn't sound like he was scolding as Kailen would have. He just sounded concerned.

"I just needed to think. I was standing over by the base of the falls when they snuck up on me, I'm sorry." I shook my head at myself. How could I be so stupid?

"Well, the next time you need to think, at least let one of us know." He gave me an encouraging smile and draped his arm around me as we made our way back to the path.

"Where did you get that sword?"

"I took it off a guard that I found lying in the tunnel." He shrugged as if it were no big deal.

"Can you use it?" I raised a brow and a devilish grin stretched across my face.

He looked offended. "Of course I can use it. I started out in the same place you did. Well, maybe not exactly the same, but I have had my share of fighter training. How else could I have survived down here this long?"

I thought about that for a minute. "Can you teach me to use it?"

He looked at me hard for a long time. "Yeah, I can teach you. After today I think you definitely need it."

13

Tuck helped me back to the cavern. It was slow going with my twisted ankle, but we finally made it.

Kailen was still inside cooking the fish on the fire when we arrived. He had never even thought about coming to check on me. My feelings were hurt again. Tuck didn't mention my ordeal to him and neither did I. I hoped that he would never find out. I had already had about all that I could take of his crazy mood swings.

I pulled myself away from Tuck and managed to walk on my own over to a large boulder. I did my best to make sure that I didn't limp. I sat down on the cool stone and tried to steady my nerves after all that had happened.

When the food was finished, it was Tuck that brought me my share. "Tomorrow when Kailen leaves to gather more supplies I will start teaching you how to fight." He whispered as he said this, so he must have been getting the same vibe from Kailen that I was.

I nodded in agreement. Kailen was leaving? He hadn't even mentioned it to me. Not that he had said anything to me since our argument the day before, other than to yell at me.

I still couldn't understand what had gone so wrong. Maybe he was bi-polar. Could fairies be bi-polar? Undoubtedly.

It had only been a few days since we shared our first kiss. I thought that maybe he really cared about me. I was certainly starting to feel something for him. I know that he was concerned that there would be no place for him in my life if I ever took over as queen, but that was just crazy. Maybe I needed to find a way to talk to him.

After we cleaned up the meal, Tuck went to lie down on his blanket on the floor. I had to take my chance while I had it. Kailen was stirring the coals around in the fire pit as I approached.

"Kailen?" He didn't bother to look up.

"Kailen, what's going on? Why are you ignoring me? I don't know what has happened between us, but I can't stand this." I pleaded.

He turned from me and walked over to the few cooking utensils that were stacked close to where we normally ate.

"Kailen!" I caught him by the arm.

"Callie, just let it go." He jerked his arm from me.

"Kailen, what in the hell is going on?"

"I should never have kissed you, Callie. I had no right." He turned away again.

"What do you mean? I thought that you felt something for me that night above the tunnel. What possibly could have happened since then to change your mind?"

"Callie, you are going to be a queen. I am just a carpenter from a village of outcasts. This could never work between us. I don't even think that I want it to. It's better to end it now before we get caught up in something that we'll both regret."

"This is really stupid Kailen!" I yelled. I just couldn't take it anymore. "If I am going to be some *queen*, then I have the right to be with whoever I choose."

"It doesn't work that way, Callie. The nobles of Petrona would never approve. They wouldn't respect you. I couldn't have that."

"So you're just going to push me away. You are not even willing to try?" I was exasperated. "You're being a real jerk Kailen."

He just stood there and glared at me for a moment. I huffed in frustration and when he didn't speak, I turned and walked away.

I laid down on my blanket and cried myself to sleep for the second night since coming here.

By the time that Tuck woke me up the next morning Kailen was already gone. I looked over to see that even his bedroll was missing.

"Is Kailen coming back?'" I asked Tuck as he straightened out his sleeping area.

"Yeah, but it will be a few days. He is going back to Drake to get a bunch of stuff so that we can start making this place more livable."

I hadn't realized that he was going to be gone that long. He didn't even have the decency to mention any of this, or to even say goodbye.

I had to stop letting him get to me like this.

Pushing him from my mind, I turned back to Tuck. "What are our plans for today?"

"Today, we teach you to fight." He said with a grin.

Tuck stood in the center of the room. He had been trying to teach me to fight using my legs. "Aim for my hands." He held his palms out to me.

I spun around with my leg in the air and kicked him hard in the hip. It was all that he could do to keep from losing his balance.

"Nice try, but next time aim a little higher."

I tried again and this time I hit my target. It felt great. I was finally getting the hang of it. I dared Sty, or anybody else for matter, to mess with me again.

Tuck took me through exercise after exercise. I practiced kicks and punches until I didn't think that I was going to be able to lift my arms or my legs again, ever.

"Okay Callie, that's enough for today. You did good." He gave me an evil grin. "Tomorrow we really fight."

I looked at him in alarm. "You me I actually have to fight you? Like, for real?"

"Yes." He laughed. "You have to learn to block a hit, and how to counter attack once you have been blocked."

"Alright." I said with a sigh.

Tuck just laughed some more. "Right now, you need to learn how to fish."

I let a long groan.

"You need to be able to survive without me around, Callie."

"Are you planning on going somewhere?" I asked.

"No, but you never know. Plus, you can keep me company while I try to get us something fresh to eat. That jerky stuff is disgusting."

"Well, you are right about that."

We headed out to the river. Tuck pulled some string and a few hooks from his bag. He looked around on the floor for a moment and then he pounced.

"What are you doing?" I was getting a little nervous.

"Getting us some bait." He smiled as he held up a big brown beetle.

"That's really disgusting." I scrunched my nose.

He baited the hooks and we spent the next couple of hours trying to entice the fish.

"You know Callie?" He had just finished pulling his third fish from the water. "It's really going to be great when you get to be queen."

"What makes you say that?"

"You really seem to care about everyone. It really seems to bother you when someone is not happy. It would not be about the power or control to you. You would have everyone's best interest in mind, no matter what you tried to do."

"The only reason that I am even considering it is because that's what my parents wanted for me. And after seeing the people of Drake shunned from the city, and you living out here the way that you were, I knew that I needed to do something."

"Things just haven't been the same since your parents left." He looked thoughtful for a moment.

"What was it like?"

"Once Lilith forced herself into the role, she started making all of these crazy rules. They made it impossible for the poorer people to sell their merchandise. Then she started adding these crazy taxes. The ones that couldn't afford to pay were kicked out of the city."

"Wow." I said as I shook my head in disbelief.

"Some of the people that had been outcast tried to revolt. There was a great war between the outcasts and the Guard."

"Many Fae lost their lives, my parents included. They just didn't have the training or the resources to take on the queen's henchmen. Most of the remaining outcasts settled in Drake or roamed the tunnels. I'm not even sure what happened to the rest of them."

"That's really sad. It helps me to understand why I really need to do this, but I am afraid that there will have to be another war. I just don't know if we will be able to get people to fight with us again. They have already lost so much. What if we don't win? What if I can't overthrow Lilith? Won't that make things worse?"

"We will just have to win, Callie. Everything depends on it." He looked more serious that I had ever seen him look.

I never realized that getting Lilith out of Petrona would mean so much to so many Fae. I was willing to bet that there were plenty of people still living in the city that would stand beside us as well. Now I really knew that I had to do everything I could to prepare for a fight.

Tuck managed to catch a few more fish before we made our way back. We cooked them and went to bed early. I needed as much rest as I could get. My body was worn out from everything that I had put it through lately and I still had a lot left to learn.

The next day I found myself toe to toe with Tuck. I tried hard to get a hit in on him but he blocked me every time. When I wasn't paying attention, he would get a good hit in on me. I flinched with the pain of each blow, but he wasn't really hitting me hard. I am sure he could have done a lot more damage than that.

It didn't take long for my reflexes to kick in. Soon, I was giving him a run for his money. He came at me with a jab and I blocked him with my left hand as I landed a blow with my right.

I learned to roll away and get back on my feet quickly. I even learned to use my wings to fly at him to land a blow. I was quite proud of myself.

"That's it, let's call it a day." He was wiping sweat from his brow.

I bent over with my hands braced on my knees and panted to catch my breath. "Sounds good to me. What should we do the rest of the day?"

"I think that we are going to take a little trip ourselves." He winked as he said it.

A trip? I was really starting to get excited. "Where are we going?"

"There is somebody that you need to meet." He would not say anything further, which left me anxious but thrilled all at the same time. I trusted Tuck, and I knew that whatever he had up his sleeve had to be good.

We gathered a few things to take with us. Since we were setting out so late, we needed to be prepared to spend the night away from the cavern.

Once everything was ready we headed out past the waterfall, but we didn't climb back up to the tunnel. Instead, we followed the river downstream. We walked for a long time, and soon I started noticing pieces of wood tacked up all over the place. They had warnings painted in sloppy red paint. Things like *beware* and *turn back now* were positioned every few feet.

"Should we be down here?" I asked getting a little nervous.

"Yeah, you'll see." Is all that Tuck answered.

I trudged on, but I couldn't help but get a little nervous about all of the warnings.

The passage began to get wider and I began to notice random pieces of junk piled up along the walls. There were old wooden crates and broken chairs. I saw an old broken bicycle and even an old stove like the one that I used to have back home. Pretty much anything that you could imagine.

I noticed the golden glow of candle light up ahead of us. I started to slow my pace but Tuck just motioned for me to keep up.

"There it is." He started to trot ahead of me.

"Hello?" He called. "Mr. Biggins?"

I heard someone stirring as we approached a room built into the side of the wall. A short stocky man with short tattered black pants and a dirty tan button down shirt and bare feet stepped out of the doorway. He squinted his eyes at us. Then his face revealed a glint of recognition.

"Tuck? Is that you?" He asked as he came out into the passage.

"It's me." Tuck held out his hand and Mr. Biggins took it in his and shook.

"I have brought someone to meet you. This is Callie." Tuck gestured to me.

Mr. Biggins squinted again as if he were trying hard to get a good look at me.

"Well you don't say. Miss Calliope Rose." He said in awe as he shook my hand as well. "What a pleasure."

"How do you know my name?" I had never laid eyes on him before. I was sure that I would have remembered him.

"Well, you have certainly grown since the last time that I saw you, but I could never forget a face like that. You look just like your mother."

I didn't know what to say, so I just smiled. He knew my mother. That could not be a bad thing, could it?

"Come in, come in." He motioned for us to enter his room.

Inside, it turned out, was some sort of a workshop. There were tools and scraps of metal and wood strewn about a long table. In the back of the room was a small bed, a few chairs, and a few shelves covered in various half completed projects it appeared.

"Mr. Biggins, I was hoping that you could help Callie. I have been helping her learn to fight. She's come a long way and I think that she might be ready to try her hand at a good weapon."

"A weapon?" I was obviously shocked. Tuck and Mr. Biggins turned to look at me briefly, but then carried on as if I had not said anything at all.

"A weapon suitable for princess?" Mr. Biggins thought out loud. "I think that I have just what she needs." He walked over to a large wooden crate and began to root through it, tossing things here and there. "Ah, here it is."

He lifted a long wooden box that was carved with flowers and vines in intricate detail. He sat the box on the table and loosened a little golden clasp on the front of it. He raised the lid to reveal a beautiful silver sword. It was at least three feet long, and very slender. It shined like a mirror, and the handle was made of gold and was carved with the same intricate floral detail as the box. Next to it laid a long stiff leather sheath.

"Wow, this is for me?" I asked as I gazed at the beautiful blade.

"This was your mother's. She left it with me for safekeeping. Now it belongs to you." He carefully lifted it from the box with two hands and held it out to me.

I took it from him, holding it carefully by its handle. I clasped it with both hands and stepped into a warrior's pose. "How do I look?"

Tuck laughed. "Fierce. Definitely fierce."

I carefully laid the sword back on its velvety bed and closed up the box.

"How could I ever repay you?" I asked the old man.

"Just help us get our home back."

14

Tuck and I made our way back out of the passage toward the waterfall. Tuck carried my sword in its box on his back. He had wrapped it with some heavy cord and tied it across himself.

"So you can teach me to use it?" I was getting excited. I imagined myself swinging the long sword around like a ninja.

"Yes, but we need to find somewhere else for you to do it. I don't want to lose my head." He smiled.

We made it about halfway to the falls when we decided to stop for the night. Tuck wrapped the box in one of the blankets and used it as a pillow. Just in case, someone came along and tried to steal it.

The thought of that made me shiver. But I felt pretty safe here with Tuck.

We settled onto our beds and I laid there in the dark for a long time. Sleep never found me. I found myself wide awake worrying about what kind of queen I would possibly make.

My parents never explained any of this to me. They raised me as a normal human girl not a princess. How was I supposed to rule a whole kingdom?

The thought of it made me want to laugh. It was like I was transported into the pages of book. No a fairy tale. That definitely made me smile.

The first thing that I would do, I thought, would be to let the outcasts back into the city. Maybe I could make Drake a part of my kingdom too, and maybe even our cavern if anyone wanted to live there.

Where would I want to live? The thought of going back to that dreadful palace made me cringe. I definitely did not want to live there. Then again, my parents had built it. Maybe I could do something to it to make it more livable and less like Lilith. I could open it up so that my new friends like Tuck could live there too. Maybe it wouldn't be so bad.

I don't think that I had slept very long when I felt Tuck nudging me awake. "We better get going."

We gathered our things and a short time later, we entered the cavern.

Kailen still had not returned. I tossed my pack down and began unpacking things and setting them back up for later. Tuck built a fire and we ate a few vegetables that we had left over from my stop in Drake.

"Are you ready to try this baby out?" Tuck asked with a gleam in his eye as he held up the box containing my sword.

"Absolutely." I took the sword out, it felt amazing in my hands. I immediately leapt into a warrior pose and grinned.

Tuck laughed and put me through several exercises. My arms ached from swinging it over and over again, but he would never let me give up. He just kept pushing me.

"There are no time outs in battle, Callie. You have to build up your strength."

He was right. I stretched out my muscles and began again. I soon started to feel like the Karate Kid. Wax on, wax off, as I took swing after swing. I kept it up until I thought that I would collapse. Then, I called it a day.

The next day Tuck said that, he had to go out for a while, and that I should stay behind and practice. I tried to protest, but he promised that he would not be gone long.

I ran through my exercises, but my heart wasn't in it. It was not nearly as much fun when I had to do it by myself. Before long, I gave up and plopped down onto the cold floor.

My stomach started growling and I tried to think of something to cook besides fish. The only problem was that there is nothing down here except bugs and rats. What I wouldn't give for a nice juicy cheeseburger or a greasy slice of pizza.

I opted for a piece of jerky. No cooking required, and since it was just me, there was no point in going through the trouble.

When Tuck finally returned he was pulling a large wooden cart. It had large spoked wheels and a thick rope that he used as the handle.

In the back of the cart, there was a table with four legs and several wooden ladder backed chairs.

Sitting toward the front of the cart was a girl. She appeared to be close to my age, she had long wavy dark hair and deep brown eyes. She had a small heart shaped face, and when she smiled, she reminded me of what I always imagined fairies to look like when I was a little girl. Her long slender wings were shades of pink with a touch of pale green.

"I thought that you could use some company." Tuck grinned as he started to unload the cart. "This is Jenna Salvia. She has been living out here on her own for a while too."

I introduced myself to Jenna with a shy little wave.

"Tuck is usually pretty good about checking in on me. I was beginning to wonder what happened to him." She smiled at Tuck, and he smiled back. I thought maybe I saw a spark of something pass between them. It would be good for Tuck to have somebody like Jenna.

Seeing the two of them together just made me think of my own lonely fate. I was beginning to think that I was destined to spend the rest of my life alone. I was somehow strangely bonded to Brokk. My heart still skipped a beat whenever I thought of him. I was supposed to marry him someday but I really wasn't sure about that.

He turned out to be a real jerk. Then, I started to have feelings for Kailen, and now he didn't want anything to do with me. I was beginning to think that maybe I had been cursed.

I helped Tuck and Jenna unload the wagon. We set up the table and chairs close to the fire pit.

Tuck brought over a tall shelf and stood it against one wall. Here he stacked several cooking utensils along with a bunch of clay dishes. He carried two large buckets out to the river and filled them with water.

I stood back and looked around. This place was really starting to come together. "Where did you find all of this stuff?" I asked turning to Tuck.

"It belongs to Jenna. When I told her about this place she got really excited and so we loaded up her wagon with some of her things and here we are." He draped an arm over Jenna's shoulder.

"I hope that you don't mind." Jenna smiled. "I just thought it would be nice to be around real live people again. It gets awfully lonely out there in the tunnels."

"I don't mind at all." I smiled back. "I am ecstatic to have a girl here. It's not easy living with just the guys to talk to." We both giggled at that.

"I'm going back to Jenna's old place to get the rest of her things. You two can stay here and get to know each other." Tuck said as he pulled the cart back out of the cavern.

Jenna and I sat and talked for hours.

We even came up with a name for the cavern. We decided to call it Maricela, which in Spanish translates to something along the lines of rebel heaven. It was perfect.

Jenna told me the story about how she ended up in the tunnels. It was very similar to Tuck's. She lost her family to the guards and found herself on her own at a very young age. She met Tuck a while back and they somehow managed to keep tabs on each other.

"You know, the best thing about being a girl," Jenna asked as she got to her feet. "We can do all sorts of things that the guy fairies can't do."

I was taken back. "What do you mean?"

"We are more in touch with the elements. We can call on their sprits when we need to and they respond to us."

"What are you talking about? What are the elements?" I was really starting to get confused. Was she saying that I could talk to spirits?

"Callie, there are four elements in nature. They are what really rule the earth."

I was still puzzled. When I didn't say anything, she continued.

"There is fire, earth, air, and water. Each of these elements is magical in its own unique way. Each has a spirit that rules over it. You can summon that magic using the spirit whenever you need to."

"Why would I need to summon them?" I was still perplexed.

"Here I'll show you." She said as she stood up and faced the fire pit. She closed her eyes and after a moment, she began. "I call you Brenton, spirit of fire, to light this wood so that I may warm this room and prepare our meal."

I looked to the fire pit and a large burst of flames rose up. I could feel the warmth of it on my face. I could hardly believe it. I wasn't sure if I should laugh or run in fear.

"Thank you Brenton." Jenna said opening her eyes. She turned and smiled at me. "You see? Easy."

I didn't know what to say. "Wow, Jenna. That was amazing." I finally managed.

"You just have to concentrate, and ask the spirit for what you need. Just remember to thank them when you finish."

"So you really think that I can do that?"

"I know that you can. I bet that you are probably more in touch with them than I am. You could probably summon them without even thinking once you got the hang of it."

Jenna agreed to help me learn to use the elements myself. With her guidance, I was able to call on the water spirit, Naida. She and I actually made it rain inside the cave. I used Erion the air spirit to summon a breeze to stir Jenna's hair around her face. I think she was just as amused as I was.

Demi, the earth spirit, caused the ground to rumble and cylindrical stone rose up from the floor. Jenna sat down onto it and held out her arms and smiled.

"See? Easy."

"That was pretty amazing. I almost wet my pants when I saw Naida appear and stir up that little cloud." I laughed but Jenna just cocked her head and looked at me as if she were confused.

"Do you mean that you actually saw the spirit? Like the actual person or whatever?"

"Well, yeah. Wasn't I supposed to?" I was getting a little nervous by the look on Jenna's face. I hoped that I hadn't done something wrong.

"That's really strange, Callie. I have never met anyone that has actually witnessed the spirit before. What did they look like?"

I thought back to all that took place as I called to the spirits. I was so nervous at the time that I really did not look very closely at them. If I had known that no one else ever got to see them, I would have paid more attention.

"Well, I watched Brenton appear and light the fire when you called him. He is a pretty big guy, very muscular. He's kind of a ginger. He has red hair, his eyes are a glowing golden color. He has fair skin. He was probably a few years older than us, I'd say mid twenties. He was bare-chested and he had a sword strapped to his back. He had a large tattoo of flames that started at his waist and stretched up his back and neck.

Basically, he was pretty hot. No pun intended." We laughed, Jenna more in astonishment than at my lame jokes.

"What about the others?" I could tell she was getting excited.

"Demi was very dark complected, almost Latino maybe? She had long dark hair, and dark eyes. She was wearing a long flowing green dress. The back was open and revealed a tattoo of a tree with a think trunk and branches that reached up to her shoulders."

"So basically they are all tatted up?" She giggled.

"Yeah, pretty much. Erion was tall and slender but with lots of chiseled muscles. He had short spiky blonde hair and pale blue eyes. He didn't bother with a shirt either. Which was nice. No tattoos for him. Naida was tall and thin. She has long straight coal black hair and deep blue eyes. She wore a long colorful sarong around her waist and a top that just came up over one shoulder. "

"Wow, that's amazing. I have never met anyone that has been able to see them before. I wonder what it means?" Jenna was making me a bit nervous, but I brushed her off. I wanted to play some more.

We practiced a while longer and each time that I called one of the elements, it seemed to get easier and easier.

After a while, it felt as if I had become one with them. Like they were now a part of me and I was a part of them. They just knew what I wanted and were already there when I tried to call them.

I smiled at Demi when she appeared to help me grow an apple tree under one of the holes in the roof. When she saw me look directly at her, she cocked her head as if she were confused. She slowly started to approach and when she saw that I was still watching her she smiled. She even did a little dance of excitement before she disappeared.

"What are you girls up to?" Tuck asked from the doorway.

"I was just showing Callie a few tricks." Jenna said with a smile.

Just then, a small cloud appeared over top of Tuck's head and began to shower him with cool raindrops.

We all laughed until our sides hurt and I finally asked it to go away.

"Were you able to get all of my stuff?" Jenna was already rooting through the wagon.

"Oh yeah. This is the last of it." Tuck moved toward the cart and helped her unload some stuff.

Jenna picked a spot a little ways away from where I usually slept and Tuck helped her to set up her small bed. She tucked her things away in a tall dresser that she had set up against the wall.

"All set?" I asked.

"Yup, it feels like home already." She smiled and fell back onto her bed.

"Tomorrow we can try to gather some wood. We could tie them together to form some walls, that way we can have some privacy." Tuck was already planning how we would make our new place into a home.

"That would be great." I had not had a moment of privacy since I got there. It would be nice to have my own little place to call home. Even if it was just a few little walls. It would also be nice to have a real bed. The stone floor was no substitute.

That night Tuck moved his things closer to Jenna's and I was left feeling very alone. I made up my mind that I would talk to Kailen one last time, and if he still wouldn't listen then I would have to push him out of my mind. I was growing very tired of felling hurt and alone all the time.

15

The next day was spent with Jenna. She sparred with me as Tuck watched, he really enjoyed playing referee. Then she showed me a few moves that I hadn't yet seen using the sword. We even spent a little time playing with the elements and flying around the cavern.

We were in the middle of practicing the ability to summon the element spirits while flying when I heard, "Oh not again."

I nearly fell to my death when I looked and saw that it was Kailen that spoke. He was standing near the sleeping area and staring up at me. He did not look happy. I hurried to land taking extra care not to make a fool of myself. Jenna was right at my side.

Erion saw what was happening and looked very annoyed. He was helping to learn to fly faster by pushing the wind against my wings. He gave me a hard disapproving stare before he vanished.

"Is something wrong?" I asked with my arms folded across my chest.

"Why do you insist on doing things that you know are dangerous?" He sounded like he was lecturing a spoiled child. I could feel heat creeping up the back of my neck and I was sure that my face was turning bright red with anger.

"You will not speak to me that way!" I yelled, I just couldn't help it. Enough was enough.

"Yes, your majesty." He sounded cocky and gave an exaggerated bow. When he rose, he didn't look at me. Instead, he turned to Jenna.

"And who may I ask are you?" He sounded very sarcastic.

"I'm Jenna." She said in her normal overly perky tone. "You must be Kailen." She held her hand out to him.

He shook it briefly. With one eyebrow raised he asked, "And what is it that you are doing here?"

"I'm an old friend of Tuck's. He invited me to come and stay with you guys. I'm helping Callie with her magic."

"Her magic?" He huffed in disbelief. "What magic? I have spent weeks with her and I have not witnessed any magic."

I was really starting to get mad after that little statement. In fact I was about to punch him in his nose, but Jenna grabbed my arm and held me back.

"I don't know what your problem is Kailen. But you better watch your tone. I thought you were a nice guy when I first met you, but obviously I was mistaken."

"The only problem that I see here is that you have gone behind my back and started flying and using fairy magic. And to top it off you have invited a complete stranger to come and live here without my permission."

"Without your permission?" I sputtered, I didn't know how much longer I was going to be able to control myself. "Who do think you are? I don't need your permission to do anything! In case you have forgotten, I am the princess here!"

With that, I called to the elements and a hard rain came down on top of Kailen's head. I just couldn't help myself.

I caught a glimpse of Naida snickering as she dissolved away.

"Maybe now you can go cool off." I screamed as Jenna tugged me away.

"What's with that guy?" She whispered.

"I don't know." I said and went on to tell her how I had first met Kailen and about the night above the tunnel. "Now this is what I have to deal with. He's like Jekyll and Hyde."

"That is very strange, Callie. I wonder what's caused him to change so quickly. Or maybe he was really just a jerk all along. You better watch out for him."

"I don't know, but I can tell you for sure that I have had enough." I was still angry at Kailen for the way that he treated me, but at the same time, I was very sad. I thought that he was someone that I could really trust, but now he was really starting to scare me.

There was a lot of commotion just outside of the entrance to the cavern. Jenna and I turned to see what could be causing it. I was shocked to see several people emerge.

Some were carrying large over stuffed backpacks, while others pulled large wagons similar to the one that Tuck had used.

There were at least two dozen of them in all. Men and women. Some of them I recognized from Drake.

Kailen must have invited them to come back with him. And he had the nerve to ask me why I didn't seek his permission before we invited Jenna?

Kailen entered behind them hefting yet another wooden cart piled with things. I had not even noticed that he went back out. He pointed in our direction, and told the newcomers to find a place to set up camp along the wall near where we were standing. We quickly moved out of the way.

One by one, the newcomers made their way over to me and introduced themselves.

There were several couples, some with children. The first was Foster and Tania. He was short but thin with dark hair and a pointy chin. Tania, his wife, was pretty and petite. She had long strawberry blonde hair and two small children hid behind her as she spoke. They were both boys. Tanner was five and dark haired like his dad, while Tad was only three. He had pudgy cheeks and fair hair like his mother.

Next came Dain and Shaylee. Dain was tall and witty, while Shaylee was shy but lovely with soft golden curls and a friendly smile.

They had only one child, a bold and daring nine year old girl named Avery. Avery had red hair and a large patch of freckles spread across her nose and onto her cheeks.

"You don't look much like a princess." Avery said with her hands on her hips.

"Well, what should a princess look like?" I stifled a giggle.

She thought for a moment and then shrugged. "I don't know but not like you." Then she took off skipping about the cave.

I nodded and introduced myself to each one as they made their way about the cave setting up camp. Some had tents that were made of cloth while others made a bed in the back of their wagon on or on the ground.

The cavern soon filled with the chatter and laughter of its new residents. I wondered where Tuck, Jenna, and I would practice our fighting. Our open space was becoming very limited.

"Callie?" Asked an older woman named Celia. "Do you think that you could help me plant a garden, the sunlight over here should be just enough for my plants to grow." She held out a bag of seeds.

"Sure." I loved the idea of having fresh veggies. It would be great to have something to eat besides jerky and fish.

I summoned earth and asked her to bring forth a bed of rich soil.

The ground rumbled and everyone turned to stare as rich black earth heaped up from under the hard rocky floor. "Thank you Demi." I said quietly.

Celia stared at me with wide eyes and I took the bag of seeds and helped her plant little rows of vegetables. It was tedious work and I was getting dirt caked under my fingernails, but it was relaxing and gave me plenty of time to think.

"You are going to be a very powerful fairy." She said as she bent over to bury another seed.

I looked at her puzzled. "I thought all of the female Fae could summon the elements."

"No not all of them. The ones who can call them are usually only able summon one of the elements, not all four. It takes a very powerful Fairy to be able to do that."

I looked over to where Jenna was sweeping up the dust from around her little room. I watched her get frustrated and then I saw Erion appear and send a soft wind to blow the dust from Jenna's space out into the tunnel.

He turned and winked at me before he left. Even though Jenna couldn't see him, I knew that she must be pretty powerful too. I wondered if she knew about all of the things that Celia was saying. I also wondered what it was that made her so powerful.

It made sense that I would be able to call them, since I was some type of royalty or whatever.

Jenna had never really mentioned her family, other than how they died, but she was definitely able to summon all of them. I wish that I knew who her mother was.

"And I have never seen anything like this before." Celia pulled my attention back from Jenna and motioned to the garden. "You brought fertile soil through the rock floor of a cave. That's just amazing."

I smiled, but I was starting to feel a little uneasy. I had not realized that what I had done was anything extraordinary. It was something that I assumed all fairies could do. Then again, why would she need my help if she could have done it herself?

I couldn't help but smile to myself as I imagined what her reaction would be if she knew that I could actually see and interact with the sprits. She might just faint.

Celia went back to her work. She planted row after row of corn, beans, squash, and a bunch of other vegetables. We would definitely have ourselves a feast when they were grown. When she was through, I called on Naida the water spirit to bring a gentle shower to water her crops. I thought she would wet her pants from laughing so hard as she watched the little rain cloud gliding over her garden.

She thanked me repeatedly, and I promised to come back every day and water the plants until they were ripe.

I walked back to Jenna's room, which was actually coming along pretty nicely. Tuck had worked all day on building her walls. The wooden slats while not entirely solid still created a nice sense of privacy and personal space.

"This is great!" I said to Tuck as he finished attaching a narrow door with thick leather straps.

"Thanks Callie! Tomorrow I'll get started on yours." He looked up and wiped some sweat from his brow. Poor guy. He was really working hard to turn this place into a home. It was good to see him actually find somewhere that he truly felt like he belonged, but I hated that he was having to work so hard to make it right.

"That sounds nice Tuck, but I don't even have a bed. It's really not necessary."

"Didn't Kailen tell you?" He stood up looking confused.

"Tell me what?" Kailen had not said a nice word to me in nearly a week.

"He brought you a bed back from Drake. It's right over there." He pointed to a stack of wood and an old mattress that had been propped up against the wall. "When I get through here, I will come and put it together for you."

"Okay, great! I'll clear a spot to set it up." That really had me smiling.

"Just let me know when you are ready."

I looked around for a good place to have my room. I wanted to move as far away from Kailen as possible, but I did not want to be on the other side of the cavern with people that I didn't really know.

"Can I have the spot on the other side of Jenna? Or were you planning to use that spot?" I raised an eyebrow at him.

"Nope you can have it." He said with a chuckle. "I was planning to set up over here between Jenna and the wall."

With that settled, I went to inspect my new bed. It was a little scuffed and dirty so I found an old rag and I got a bucket of soap and water from one of the newcomers. I scrubbed the bed from top to bottom. I even wiped down the mattress, but it still had a funny odor. I was standing there staring at it when I heard someone say, "Why don't you call to earth to make it smell like flowers?"

It sounded like a great idea, so I closed my eyes and summoned Demi to fill my mattress with the scent of lilacs. Suddenly the whole room smelled like fresh flowers and when I put my nose to the mattress, it smelled just like fresh cut lilacs.

"That was pretty amazing." The voice said again. I turned to see who was speaking, only to find Kailen standing a few feet behind me.

"Did you need something?" I asked with indifference.

"Callie, I just wanted to apologize for the way that I have been acting."

"Don't bother." I said as I tried to walk away. Kailen caught me by the arm, and I was stopped in my tracks. I should have pulled away from him but I just didn't have the energy anymore.

"Please Callie. Just hear me out." He was trying to meet my eyes.

I let out a long heavy sigh. I tried to fight it but I couldn't. I looked up to meet his eyes. "Go ahead."

"Callie, I never meant to hurt you. I recognized who you were immediately when you walked into Drake. You were beautiful and kind, but you were never meant to be with someone like me. I tried to keep my distance. That night in the hollow, I let my emotions get the best of me. I should not have kissed you. I should have stopped it right then, but I was not sure of what I should say. You are our future queen Callie. You need to focus on your future, not on me."

This guy's ego was bigger than I thought. "Okay Kailen. Whatever. I really don't know why you would say that I need to focus on being a queen when you have admonished everything that I have tried to do."

"Callie, what are you talking about?" He was turning red in the face.

"You got mad because I was trying to learn to fly, then you blew up because I was using the spirits. You said that I should have waited for you, but you have done nothing to help me since we left Drake. I am really starting to feel like you are just full of it. I don't even know what else to say to you."

He just stood there shaking his head.

"Well, thanks for the bed. I guess I'll see you around."

I tried again to walk away. This time he let me go. I guess that I should have been hurt, but after the last week, I was just pretty much numb. I was sick and tired of all of the mixed signals that he was tossing at me. It just wasn't fair and the truth was that I didn't really know him at all. He was nothing like the person that I thought that he was when we first met. I was beginning to wonder what I ever saw in him at all.

16

"Callie!" Jenna called from across the cave. I looked up from where I was weeding the garden to see her waiving at me to join her.

I walked over to where Jenna was standing with several of the people from Drake. They seemed to be having a serious discussion about the royal guards. Apparently, the guards had been frequently coming into Drake and causing all sorts of problems.

"They kicked down the door and tore everything apart inside of the house. They our broke our furniture and tore up all of our clothes. It was a mess." I heard Dain say.

"That's right, and they destroyed Marlan's workshop just the other day. He had nothing left. They even took his tools." Said another.

"What do they want?" I asked and they all turned to look at me.

"It is really nothing for you to concern yourself with princess. Everything will be fine." Dain said with an uneasy smile.

"Look, I am not some scared little girl that you have to protect. You cannot keep things like this from me. Tell me what's going on." I was starting to get really irritated with this whole princess business.

"It seems as if the queen has discovered that the outcasts have settled in Drake and now she wants to control them as she controls Petrona." Jenna explained. "She is demanding that they pay her taxes and whatever they pay is never enough. She has been sending the guard to collect more money and when the citizens can't pay, they start destroying things."

"Oh no." I could not just stand by and let Lilith continually take advantage of these good people. "We have to do something!"

"What can we do?" Someone asked.

"We can't take on the royal guard." Said another.

"Why not?" I knew the Guard could be tough, but I didn't see why we couldn't take them on.

"They out number us for one thing, and they are better trained in fighting. We would be no match for them."

"We could train. We could learn to fight. We can not just sit here and let her take everything that the people of Drake have worked so hard for." I pleaded. "What if she finds Maricela? Then she will want to do the same thing here. I could never allow that."

"She is right." I looked to my right to find that this time it was Kailen who had spoken. "We must do something."

"What do you propose?" Dain turned to Kailen.

"We gather as many people as we can that are able to fight. We equip them with weapons and train them to use them. When we are ready, we could storm the city. It will not be easy, some may get hurt. But a lot more will get hurt if we continue to allow this to go on." Kailen looked fierce as he spoke.

They continued on like that for a long time. Strategies and plans were discussed. I tried to listen, but my mind kept wondering to my family. And to the families of my friends. They had all lost their lives trying to battle Lilith and her Army. An army that was most likely a lot stronger by now. I could not let any more people die trying to fight for something that they never should have lost.

If it weren't for me, and what my mother did to protect me, Lilith would never have been able to take over as queen. The war never would have happened. There never would have been outcasts.

No, I needed to do something. I needed to do something on my own. I would not allow anyone else to get hurt because of me.

"Jenna?" I asked. "Let's train hard today. I want you to give me all that you've got. I want to test all of my limits."

"Okay." Jenna was eyeing me skeptically. "Let's go."

We moved to the open area of the cave and started out with a little hand to hand combat.

I fought with all my might and Jenna was a little startled, but she regrouped and came back at me with as much ferocity as I was using to come at her. Sweat started to bead on my brow. I looked around and realized that we had drawn a crowd.

Tuck stepped up with that usual mischievous glint in his eye. "My turn."

He was definitely more of a match for me than Jenna, but it was exactly what I needed.

I fought even harder. As he came at me, I would back flip away from his blow and come back at him with a harder strike.

We began to use our wings as we fought. We were so high above the floor of the cavern that I was afraid that we would bump our heads on the ceiling. I even learned to somersault and do loop to loops in the air as we fought.

Jenna flew up to meet us and it became two against one. I started to get a little nervous, but I knew that I needed to learn to fight with distractions.

I watched as Jenna summoned Brenton. He appeared beside her and smiled devilishly. I knew I was in for it. He raised his hand out, palm up, and a ball of fire about the size of a baseball appeared. I knew that it was destined for me so with barely a thought I called Naida. She met his fiery orb with a cold blast of water, and then turned to Jenna and hit her with a blast too.

I nearly fell from my perch with laughter but I felt a strong gust of wind push me back up. I looked around to find Erion at my side. I hadn't even called for him.

It didn't take long for Demi to show up and join in the fun. By the time that we were through, we were all exhausted. I thanked each of the element spirits and they all bowed to me in turn before they left.

We lowered ourselves back to the floor of the cavern and were met with a roar of cheers. The new citizens of Maricela loved the display of our skills. Tuck barely made it through the crowd. He had to promise several of the men that he would teach them to fight. Jenna also began to speak to some of the women about what types of magic they possessed.

I was surprised to learn that Tanya could summon fire. She said that she had never really practiced using her magic before. She had only used it a few times to light a cooking fire.

Jenna and I would definitely have to make a note of who possessed the spirits and make sure that they knew how to use them properly. You just never know when you may need them.

We took a break from our training and went to find something cool drink. The ladies from Drake had prepared a delicious smelling lunch of roasted vegetables and fish. I had really worked up an appetite and I ate heartily.

The fish was succulent and had just the right amount of spices and the vegetables were roasted perfectly. It was nice to have something to go along with the fish for a change.

I overheard some of the people talking about how bad things had gotten in Drake since I left. I couldn't help but feel a little guilty. This whole mess was because of me. I just wished that my mother would have stayed. She could still be queen and everybody would still be happy.

A deep sadness filled me once again as I thought of my mother. I still couldn't believe that she was gone. I knew that I had to push it from my mind, but sometimes it was just so hard. I resigned that the only way to honor her and my dad was to keep fighting for what was right. I knew then that I would have to work even harder to put a stop to Lilith.

After lunch, Tuck and I were back at it. We drew our swords and went at it like a couple of swashbuckling pirates. It was a little tricky because I didn't really want to hurt him. We battled ruthlessly as our swords clanked repeatedly sending loud echoes throughout the cave.

Tuck smiled at me during a brief pause in our battle. "You have really been practicing."

"I want to be ready for the fight." I raised my sword into an attack stance.

"It looks like you will be." He answered as he rounded me with his own blade.

Later that evening after everyone had gone to bed, I snuck out into the cave and stretched out my wings. I still needed to be sure that I had the whole flying thing down. It always made me very nervous. I started to think that my fear was stemming from Kailen's repeated scolding whenever I tried to use them and I definitely couldn't have that.

I propelled myself to the roof of the cavern and carried myself up to the large holes that opened just enough to let sunlight shine onto our garden. From there I found that I could stay very still while remaining in the air. I peered out into the night.

The sky was lit in a beautiful array of starlight. I tried to pick out the constellations and I thought that I saw a shooting star. It was absolutely amazing and I tried to remember the last time that I had actually saw the night sky.

"Callie." Someone whispered. I nearly fell to the ground but I caught myself immediately. I was quite proud of that.

I looked to find Kailen once again beside me. His glorious blue and green wings were spread wide as he looked into my face. I didn't know what to say. I thought that he made it very clear that he did not want to be with me.

"What is it Kailen?" I asked quietly.

"I am going to be leaving in the morning, Callie. I am going back to Drake to prepare the others. Plus, I really want to be there to help protect them when the Guard comes back." He was looking a little nervous.

I looked at him for a moment, but I didn't say a word. What did he want me to say?

"I just wanted to say goodbye and that I am sorry that I hurt you." He looked to the ground in an attempt to hide the sadness in his eyes.

"It doesn't have to be this way." I had let his eyes get the better of me. "If you truly cared about me, we would find a way to make this work."

I looked at him for a while but his eyes would not meet mine.

Finally he spoke. "This could never work Callie. You are who you are, and I am just me. I am truly sorry." He started to descend. "I need to start preparing to go."

"Wait!" I called.

He held one hand up to me and I took it, but slowly he continued to move away. My hand glided from his and then he was gone.

"Please, stay." I whispered into the dark.

I did not sleep any that night. I stayed gazing out at the stars for a long time. I watched Kailen as he loaded his pack onto his back and headed out into the tunnels. He only glanced back once, but I could still see the sorrow in his eyes.

Why did he have to be so stubborn?

I lowered myself onto the ground. I didn't know what else to do so I started pulling weeds from the garden as I waited on everyone else to stir. The quiet and the repetitiveness of pulling weeds left me a lot of time to think.

I decided that I could not just stand by and let another war happen. I needed to go and take care of Lilith myself. I wasn't sure what I would do about the guard, but I would cross that bridge later.

I spent the day stocking up on a few things that I would need for my journey. I had to do it a little at a time so that no one would notice.

I packed away several days worth of jerky, a few pieces of fruit, and a couple of bottles of water. I added my comb and an extra hair tie, just in case. One extra set of clothes and a small blanket went into the pack, although I had no intention of sleeping for very long.

I set my stuff under my bed hoping that no one would notice it there. I needed to try to get out with as little fuss as possible.

I went out to join the others and ate a good supper. The last thing that I needed was to be hungry when I started out. I needed to get as far as I could before anyone noticed that I was missing.

I waited until everyone had gone to bed and I could hear their soft snores. Once everything got still, I slipped into my most comfortable pair of blue jeans, a t-shirt, and thick black hooded sweatshirt. It can get pretty chilly in the tunnels at night. I slid into a pair of comfy sneakers, thanks to Kailen. He brought them back with him the last time that he had gone to Drake.

I just need one last thing. I slid the long wooden box that contained my sword from under my bed.

I admired its beauty as I pulled it from its velvety bed and slipped it into its sheath. I wrapped the leather strap across my chest and I liked the way that it felt as it hung on my back. It made me feel like some sort of samurai warrior or something.

I pulled my pack onto my shoulders. It rested against the sword but I would just have to deal with it. I needed to be able to move freely.

I crept through the cavern to the entrance and turned back one last time to look at all that I would miss so dearly. Then I stepped into the dark passage.

I felt my way along the wall and soon I was hearing the loud roar of the waterfall. As I exited the passage and started to head to the path that would lead me up to the tunnel, I saw two dark figures lurking in the corner.

I froze as flash backs of my ordeal with Sty and Sully entered my mind. I could feel my heart racing fast and I found myself reaching for my sword.

"Where do you think you're going?" A deep voice said.

I whipped my head around and the strangers approached.

Relief filled me as I realized that it was only Tuck and Jenna. Then dread started to set in as I thought that they were here to try and stop me.

"You didn't think that we would let you do this alone did you?" Jenna asked in her sweet pixie voice.

"I can't ask you guys to come with me. It's too dangerous. I need to do this on my own." I shook my head and started to walk past them, but Tuck stood in my way.

"There is no way that you are going to leave me out of all of that action." Tuck laughed.

"Give it up Callie, we're going." Jenna said firmly.

What else could I say? They had obviously already made up their mind.

"Okay, then let's go. We need get out of here before anyone notices that we are gone." I started walking again.

Jenna and Tuck slung their packs onto their back and we all headed up to the tunnel.

I made a silent wish that my friends would both be okay once the fighting started. I didn't think that I could stand to lose anyone else in my life.

17

We made our way down the slick corridor as quickly as we could without making too much noise. I could hear the sloshy sound of our footsteps reverberating off of the walls.

I let Tuck lead the way. I figured that he had spent the most time down there so he would know the way better than me.

"What is your plan once we reach Petrona?" Jenna said to me as we careened around a corner.

"I really don't have a plan. I figured that I would have time to come up with one on the way there." I smiled but she looked worried.

"Gee, you have really thought this thing through." She said sarcastically with huff.

"Well, obviously I can't take out an entire Army plus the Royal Guard by myself. I was thinking that maybe I would just try to go directly for Lilith." That was the best that I could come up with.

"You would never be able to get to her." Jenna was shaking her head. "They are all on high alert as it is. She knows that you are out here, and I am sure that she knows that you would come back eventually."

"I just don't see any other way." We trudged on in silence, each of us deep in thought about the upcoming fight.

After a few more minutes of walking through the tunnel, I thought that I heard something up ahead.

"Wait!" I whispered coming to a stop. Tuck and Jenna stopped too. "Did you hear that?"

We listened intently for a few moments.

"Sounds like voices up ahead." Tuck cupped his hand to his ear.

We help our ground as we waited to see who would approach. Two dark figures appeared before us. They stopped talking as soon as they saw us standing there.

"Well, well. It's our old friend." One of them said in a gruff voice.

They drew closer and my stomach twisted into a knot as I realized who was coming at us.

Sty and his big friend Sully walked up to us grinning.

"Well if it isn't our favorite little princes." How did they know who I was? They must have known that it was me the day that they tried to kidnap me by the waterfall.

"And look she brought along her boyfriend." Sty said as he eyed Tuck from head to toe. Tuck stiffened but he didn't make a move.

"And who this pretty little thing?" Big and ugly asked as he lifted a lock of Jenna's hair.

"Don't touch her!" I whirled on them and yelled.

They started laughing their obnoxious laugh.

"We should have never let your mother take you away from us." Sty snickered.

What was he talking about? What did this have to do with my mother?

"We almost had her Sty." Sully elbowed his friend in the ribs.

"To bad she hid you away like that, or we could have met a lot sooner." Sly was speaking right into my face. I could smell his rotten breath and I wanted to retch.

These were the rogue Fae that tried to kidnap me when I was younger? These two were the reason that my parents fled their home? Why they thought they needed to protect me? Why they were now both dead and why Lilith was in control?

My anger started boiling within me as I realized how many lives had been ruined or lost because of the actions of these two men.

I felt my fingers twitch.

"Now, princess. Won't you come with me and save your friends from a lot of pain and suffering." It was Sty who spoke but his big and ugly friend Sully snickered.

It was the last straw. I could not stand to see them roaming around free when the people of Drake had to hide.

I looked at Jenna and Tuck. Both of them lost their family to the war that started because my parents ran away from these two men and Lilith took over. Enough was enough.

More quickly than anyone could have thought, I reached up and grabbed my sword by the handle. I pulled it from its sheath still strapped to my back and swung it with deadly force.

The next thing I knew, bright red blood was spreading across the cold dark floor. Sty and his buddy lay on the ground. Their chests revealed a large gaping hole. I had nearly cut them in half.

I dropped to the floor on my knees and the sword fell from my hand and clanked loudly against the hard stone. I buried my face in my hands and wept.

I sat like that for a long time. Jenna and Tuck left me alone while they moved the bodies from sight. When they were through Jenna gently held me by my arm and pulled me to my feet.

"We have to get moving Callie." She said quietly in my ear. I just nodded and began to walk.

I could not believe that I had just killed two people. It was an odd feeling. One that I hoped that I would never have to feel again, but I wasn't sure about that. I was entering into dangerous territory.

What bothered me the most is that I wasn't crying for the two men that I had just killed. I was crying for all of the people who had been made to suffer from their actions. They needed to be punished. I didn't know if this was the best way, but now it was done.

"Are you okay?" Jenna gave me a quick squeeze.

"I am going to be alright." I whispered and I knew that it had to be true. I had to focus on the battle that was quickly approaching.

A few hours later Tuck found a small alcove off of the main corridor. It was just big enough for the three of us to lie down.

"We should stop here and get some rest." He said. "You've had a long night Callie. You would feel a lot better if you could get some sleep."

We spread out our blankets and laid down. Jenna wrapped her arms around me as I lay curled into a ball. I looked back at her and noticed Tuck had his arms around Jenna. They smiled at me and I couldn't help but laugh.

It wasn't long before I could feel Jenna's arms around me go limp and I could tell by the steady sound of their breathing that they had both fallen asleep.

I couldn't help but think back to the night that I spent with Kailen's arms wrapped around me as I slept. It seemed so long ago now. I still could not believe that he turned out to be so different than I was sure that he was that night.

I thought that we had really shared something special. He helped me to remember a tiny little part of my life that I had long since forgotten.

I reached up and pulled the little gold coin from beneath my shirt. I stroked it gently between my thumb and forefinger. I had not taken it off in over ten years. I will always be with you in your heart. Those words seemed to lose their meaning now.

A single tear made a trail down my cheek. I wasn't sure if I had loved him. I really had not known him long enough to say that I did, but I kind of hoped that what we shared would turn into something. I just wished that I knew what went wrong.

I know that he said that we belonged in two separate worlds, but I really did not think that was true. His family had been the ones to help my parents when they took me away. They must have been close to my family at some point.

Thinking of my family brought my thoughts back to Brokk. He was definitely another love gone wrong.

I reached down and slid the heavy gold ring from my pocket.

Maybe I was just a little too eager to fall in love, I thought as I stared at it in the dim cavern light. The way things stand right now, I have a necklace and a ring, but no guy. It's kind of funny in a pathetic sort of way if you think about it.

After some time while lost in my thoughts, I finally managed to fall asleep. I woke several hours later to find that my friends were already awake. They were whispering quietly to each other a few feet away from me. I kept very still while I listened to them talk.

"Do you think that we are doing the right thing?" I heard Tuck ask.

"Yes, she knows what she needs to do. I just don't think she needs to try to take on a whole city alone." Jenna whispered in reply.

"I don't either. I'm glad that we came. I just hope that the three of us can pull this off."

"Me too." Jenna turned to sit up.

They were right about one thing, there was no way that I could take on the whole city and the guards. The one thing that she was wrong about was that I had no idea what I needed to do.

I still wasn't sure that I even wanted to be queen. I just wanted to help all of the outcasts. I waited for a few minutes and when they no longer spoke, I started getting up too. We quickly dressed packed away our things and headed out.

"We should make it to Drake in a few hours." Tuck advised us as he looked at our surroundings.

I'm not really sure how he could tell. Everything looked the same to me. Dark, rocky, and slick.

"I hope that no one sees us." I whispered.

The last thing that I needed was to run into Kailen. Not because I didn't want to see him, but because I knew that he would try to stop me.

"We will have to be especially careful. There may be a lot of people coming and going at this time of the day. Especially if they have already begun to gear up for a battle. They may be on high alert." Tuck warned.

"Petrona is not far from Drake. We should try to come up with what we are going to do once we get there." Jenna looked at me as she said that. "We can't just walk into town swinging a blade."

"No, you are right. We have to be careful. If the guards see me, they will know something is going on. I can't just go walking down the middle of the street. I wouldn't make it ten feet."

"Maybe we should go in at night?" Tuck suggested.

"That's a good idea, but there will still be guards posted everywhere." I just didn't see any other way to do it. At least at night there may not be as many guards.

We walked on, each deep in thought as different strategies played out in our heads. We thought of everything from wearing disguises to going in while hanging to the bottom of one of the merchant's carts.

None of these ideas were enough to eliminate the guard all together. Jenna wished that we had more manpower, but I didn't want any more people to get hurt for this cause. This was something that I needed to do without causing an all out war if at all possible.

I would definitely have to come up with something good and I would have to do it soon. It wouldn't be long until we made it to Drake and I needed a plan before then.

The last time that anyone had run into the guards they were in Drake. Apparently, they were becoming regulars there. The thought of them stealing from the villagers and destroying their homes stirred my anger once again.

Lilith would definitely have to be dealt with but the Guard needed to be stopped as well. I just might have to start thinking more seriously about becoming the queen once Lilith was out of the picture.

The thought of it scared me to death, but the fate of the people in and around Petrona worried me more. There was no longer any question of whether I wanted to be queen or not, I needed to be.

My new found purpose is all the inspiration that I needed to propel me the rest of the way through the tunnel.

I could feel my adrenaline kicked in and I was prepared to do whatever it took to finish this once and for all.

18

I spent the next couple of hours going over all of the things that would be expected of me as the queen with Tuck and Jenna. There was a lot to think about. I would have to command the Guard, make sure that the streets and the rest of the city was maintained. I would have to impose punishment on those that broke the laws, maintain a good relationship with other fairy kingdoms. The more responsibilities that they thought of the more my stomach started to churn.

"Don't worry, Callie." Tuck must have noticed my sudden tension. "You will have plenty of help. You won't have to do everything on your own."

That was a relief. I was having trouble understanding how one person could do so much.

As we approached Drake, we could hear the sound of music being played. I could hear a lot of chatter and laughter emptying out into the tunnels. The three of us moved very slowly with our backs plastered against the tunnel wall. I could feel the sharp edges tugging on my pack as we moved.

We tried to stay hidden deep within the shadows. I knew that getting past this point would be tricky, but I never expected so much commotion. It sounded as if there was a party going on inside.

"I'll be right back. I need to get some air and cool off." We heard somebody call out as footsteps began to draw near.

We froze. I did not even want to breathe. I hoped that the dark shadows of the tunnel would keep us hidden from whoever was about to step out of the doorway.

A tall familiar figure entered the tunnel, he stood just outside of the cavern and took a long exaggerated breath. I strained to get a better look at who it was that looked so recognizable but he was facing away from me. I couldn't really get a good look.

We waited. I hope that whoever it was would gather himself and just head back in to the party.

The figure turned and stretched his arms tall, and when he brought them back down his eyes locked with mine.

He squinted in the darkness of the tunnel as if he were trying to get a better look. "Callie?" He asked quietly.

"Brokk." I said in a breath. I would recognize the sound of that voice anywhere. Even now, it sent an odd heat radiating through my body. Of all the people in the world to catch us, it just had to be Brokk.

He moved toward me and I raised my arm and grabbed my sword by the handle. I didn't really think that he was about to hurt me, but I wanted to be prepared for anything.

"Callie, what are you doing out here?" He acted as if nothing had ever gone wrong between us.

"I was just about to ask you the same thing." I held his gaze and smirked, but I never took my hand from my sword.

"I left the queen. After the last time that I saw you, I realized that she was evil and I finally saw what she was doing to me. So I left Patrona and came here." He motioned toward the village behind him.

"How long have you been here Brokk?" I was getting a little irritated. He was talking to me as someone would talk to a friend that they hadn't seen in a while. Apparently, he had forgotten the way that things had ended between us.

"Since the day after our fight, the guards found me in the tunnel and took me back to the palace to recover. I overheard the queen talking to them about you. She wanted them to hunt you down and kill you. I knew then that she had gone too far. I fled that very night and I have been here ever since." He shrugged as if it were no big deal.

I wasn't sure whether I could trust him or not. He had never lied to me in the past. He did not always disclose his intentions, but he had not lied.

If what he was saying was true, then he was here when Kailen came back for supplies. Kailen must have seen him, but he said nothing. Was this why Kailen's feelings toward me had changed?

No, that couldn't be right. Kailen had changed long before he ever came back to Drake.

Now I was really starting to get mad. How dare Kailen keep this from me? Brokk was living in Drake and he did not even think that this little detail was worth mentioning? It was absolutely unbelievable.

"What is going on in there?" Jenna asked Brokk, nodding to the door.

"They are celebrating Kailen's return to Drake." Brokk said sheepishly.

"His return?" Tuck sounded just as confused as I felt.

"Yes, he announced just this morning that he would be staying for good this time, so everyone decided to celebrate. Kind of stupid if you ask me." Brokk rolled his eyes. "But those folks are always looking for a reason to party."

I didn't know what to say. Once again, Kailen had left me speechless. He never planned to return to the cavern, another fact that he failed to mention. That dull nagging pain formed within my heart again. I could feel my face start to fall so I looked to the ground in an attempt to regain my composure. I really needed to stay away from guys for a while. Apparently, I only attracted the ones that would cause me nothing but trouble.

"Callie, please don't tell me that you fell for him. Please don't tell me that you believed all of his lies." Brokk pleaded desperately.

"Lies? What lies, Brokk?" My voiced raised a pitch and crackled as I spoke revealing my emotions on the subject.

Brokk stood looking a little defeated for a few moments.

"Didn't he tell you about his family's part in all of this?" Now he was the one getting a little heated.

"He told me that they helped my parents escape with me to the surface. He said that they taught my parents how to use their fairy magic to disguise themselves. What more does he need to tell me Brokk?" I was starting to get really upset with him. If he didn't watch himself, he was going to end up with another sore nose.

"Maybe we should continue this discussion somewhere else." Jenna interrupted. "Someone could walk out of there at anytime and find us here."

Brokk looked puzzled but he led us back the way that we had come.

A little ways back down the tunnel, he ducked into a small cavern where we were less likely to be seen or heard.

"Brokk, you better start explaining yourself!" I yelled. "And you better not lie to me!"

"I have never lied to you, Callie. And I never meant to hurt you. I was trying to explain that to you before."

"Yes, at the same time that you were trying to turn me over to the queen! You are lucky that I don't just end you right now!" I yelled again.

"Callie, calm down." Jenna said softly in an attempt to soothe my nerves. "Let's just hear what he has to say. Then we can decide how much of it we believe to be true."

She met my eyes and I stared at her for a moment. Finally, I shook my head and resigned myself to behave until I had heard all that Brokk had to say.

"Continue Whelp." Jenna told Brokk.

"Callie, it is true that Kailen's family helped your parents leave. It's why they helped that he has not bothered to tell you." Brokk started but I couldn't stand it.

"What are you talking about? They were friends of my parents. They wanted to help because they thought it was the right thing to do." I stated firmly.

"Is that what he told you?"

"No, he didn't have to tell me." I said defensively.

"Callie, Kailen's parents assisted your family to the surface because they were working with Lilith. She had been trying to weasel her way into the palace for a long time. After you were nearly kidnapped, she saw her opportunity and she took it. She had several of her supporters push your parents to leave with you."

"She made them believe that what they were doing was the right thing to do. Kailen's parents were among those that secretly supported Lilith. Once your family was out of the way, Lilith could take over the throne. And she did."

"That can not possibly be true Brokk!"

"It is the truth Callie. You need to believe me."

My legs became so wobbly that I had to brace myself against the wall with my hand. Kailen's parents tricked my family so that Lilith could take over. I replayed Brokk's words over and over again in my mind. It just couldn't be true.

"What happened to Kailen's parents after Lilith took over?" I finally asked.

"Lilith thought that she could no longer trust them. She thought that if they were traitors to your family, then they would betray her too. She had them executed. Along with several others. Their children were cast out of the city. Kailen and his brothers settled here in Drake."

"What about the war?" Jenna asked.

"Anyone who dared to defy Lilith was exiled. The older of those people started the village. Eventually they banded together and tried to stop Lilith. That's when the war started. Many lives were lost and the outcasts eventually had to back down." He said.

Jenna hung her head and stared at the ground. I knew that she was missing her family and trying to come to terms with their deaths. I placed my hand on her shoulder.

We all just stood there for a few moments taking everything in.

Kailen knew all along that his parents had betrayed mine. He never said a word. Did he pull away from me because he hated my family or because he carried some sort of guilt for what his had done? If he hated me he surely would never had agreed to help me to begin with, but he left. He left for good according to Brokk.

None of this was making any sense to me. I needed to talk to Kailen. I needed to hear the truth and I needed to hear it from him.

"I need to go. I need to talk to Kailen." I said as I started to leave the cave.

"No, Callie!" Jenna pulled me back. "If you go in there they will wonder how you got here. They will question why you traveled this far on your own. They will know what we plan to do. Callie, Kailen is not going to let you leave again."

"Like hell he's not." I said as I jerked away and headed toward Drake.

19

I stormed into Drake looking for Kailen. There was definitely a major party going on. People were playing music and dancing, some were off to one side talking. There was even a large feast spread out on a long table.

I scanned the crowd for Kailen. It was difficult to pick him out of the massive crowd that had assembled.

I finally spotted him behind the food table talking to a couple of men. One looked a lot like him. It must have been one of his brothers. He had the same dark hair and hazel eyes. Even his wings were similar with varying shades of green and blue.

I had to push people out of my way as I moved across the crowded floor. I was nearly to him when he looked up and saw that I was there. His eyes grew as big as saucers.

"Callie!" He gasped.

"You and I have a lot of talking to do." I eyed him sternly.

"There is nothing left for me to say." He put down his drink.

"Do you want me to cause a scene or should we go somewhere a little more private?" I asked gesturing to the crowd.

"What's going on Kailen?" His brother asked looking alarmed.

He looked at him for a long moment. "Nothing, I'll be right back."

He grabbed me by the arm and led me to a small wooden house a short distance away that I recognized as his.

"What are you doing here, Callie?"

"That's just what I was about to ask you." I said crossing my arms over my chest.

"I told you that I was coming back here. You watched me leave." He sounded frustrated.

"You said that you were coming back to prepare everyone for a war. It looks to me like you had no intention of doing anything like that. In fact it looks like you are having a grand ole time." I yelled.

"So you followed me here to check up on what I was doing? That is ridiculous Callie!"

"That is not why I am here, but I can see now that maybe I should have followed you. What are you up to, Kailen? And why did you keep the fact that Brokk was here from me?"

"I didn't think that it was relevant." He waved my question off.

"You did not think that it was relevant for me to know that the man who kidnapped me, and then chased me in these tunnels was your new next door neighbor?"

I fought to control my temper. "Were you jealous? Were you afraid that I would run into his arms, forgetting everything he had done to me?

"I was not jealous!" He yelled. "I just did not see why it would be of any importance to you!"

"You didn't think that it was important for me to know that you took in one of enemies like a lost puppy? You didn't think I deserved to know?"

"Callie, this is stupid. None of this matters. Just go back to the cavern where you belong." He started to get up.

"Where I belong? Where you have me hidden away like some forgotten umbrella? How dare you tell me where I should go! You have done nothing but lie and deceive me since I met you. You have no right to speak to me this way!"

"What lies have I told you Callie? How have I deceived you? Do you mean that kiss? I already told you, that was a mistake!"

"You kissed him?" I heard someone say quietly from somewhere behind me. I turned to see Brokk standing just outside of the door. He looked as if I had just dealt him a heavy blow.

"This is none of your business!" Kailen yelled.

Brokk ignored him and turned back to me. "Callie, are you okay?" He asked softly.

I nodded my head, but it was Kailen who answered for me. "She is just fine! Now why don't you get out of here and mind your own business!"

"Callie is my business Kailen, and I am not going anywhere until SHE asks me to!" He yelled back.

I turned back to see that Kailen had turned three shades of red. If I didn't know any better, I would say that smoke might start pouring out of his butt at any minute.

Kailen turned to me and I could tell that he was struggling to get his temper under control.

"Why don't you tell her the truth now, Kailen." Brokk said quietly.

Kailen just stared at me. I watched as he slowed his breathing and regained his composure completely.

When I was sure that he had calmed down, I asked my questions again. "Did your parents deceive my family so that Lilith could take over the throne?"

"Yes." He said. It was barely audible but I heard him anyway.

"What did you have to gain by leading me to the cavern and then leaving me there?"

"I thought you could live out your life there. I thought that you would be satisfied to live there, and maybe even start your own kingdom. Then you could leave Petrona and Drake in peace." He said.

"It was you who pushed me to want to be queen." This was all so confusing. "I never wanted that."

"I was only trying to appeal to you. I knew that you didn't want it, and I was counting on your fear of Lilith to keep you away. I mentioned the title to you a few times so that you wouldn't suspect what I was up to but I never planned to let you try to take over as queen." He said.

"I guess your little plan backfired on you, didn't it."

"We just want to be left in peace. I knew that you would cause trouble the first day that I saw you. You brought the royal guards here. They were chasing you and in doing so, they found us. There has been nothing but trouble since that day. Our village has been ransacked. They steal our money, our belongings, anything they can get their hands on to cover their stupid tax! Another war would be devastating to us! Can't you see that Callie?" He pleaded. "You have already cost us enough! You need to go back to the cave and stay there!"

"I never intended to cause anyone harm and you know that. I was just scared and hurt. I had just found out that my parents had been murdered. You led me out into the tunnels and you just planned on leaving me out there. Defenseless. That is why you were so angry when you saw me trying to fly. You didn't want me to be able to take care of myself. You never intended on staying. You were just going to leave me there for Tuck to take care of. You were just trying to get rid of me!"

"I thought that you would be satisfied to start your own kingdom. That is why I brought the others when they wanted to come. You could still be a queen. You could still have your own kingdom, and you could leave us in peace." He said getting firm again.

"You have really underestimated me, Kailen." I drew back my fist and landed a solid blow directly to the middle of his face. He fell backward over his small couch and landed onto his back on the floor. A trickle of blood ran from his nose.

"That's for making me waste my first kiss on a low life like you!"

I stormed out of his house and pushed my way through the crowd. I glanced up just long enough to see Kailen's brother watching me, then he quickly turned and headed for the shack. I kept going. I didn't stop until I was back in the tunnel.

Brokk was at my heels the entire way. He really was like a little lost puppy.

"What happen, Callie?" Jenna asked as soon as I stepped back into the cave.

"She beat the hell out of him!" Brokk answered.

"I was not talking to you, Dog!" She yelled and turned back to me.

"Brokk was right. He was lying about everything. He never intended on helping me get rid of Lilith. In fact it would have suited him just fine if I never would have made it back out of the tunnels." I explained as tears started to burn my eyes.

Jenna wrapped me in a strong hug and I fought to keep my tears from spilling over.

"I think that he would have been happy if I had been killed right along with my parents. I can't help but wonder about the time when I fell into the river or when I was being attacked by Sty and Sully. It was always Tuck who rescued me."

We all looked up at Tuck then.

"I don't know. That day on the river, he just climbed across the shallow end. He never really got in any hurry. I had to scramble to find some way to get you out. I can't imagine that he would have just let you drown, but he didn't really make any attempt to save you either."

"He never bothered to check on me the day that Sty and Sully found me either. If it hadn't been for you, who knows what might have happened to me."

I could feel my anger beginning to boil. How could I not have realized any of this sooner. Now that I looked back on everything, it was always Tuck coming to my rescue. Kailen never did anything. Even before we met Tuck, I fought Brokk by myself while he hid in the passage. He had never even once tried to defend me.

"He is definitely not who we thought that he was, that much is for sure." Jenna said.

"What's our plan now?" Tuck asked.

"Kick some royal butt, of course." I said with a grin.

"What should we do with him?" Jenna asked, nodding toward Brokk.

"I have already lost Callie once. Actually twice, but I am not about to lose her again." Brokk said in a growl.

I really had no idea what to do with him. The only people that I truly trusted at that point were Tuck and Jenna. Everyone else has betrayed me in some way, including Brokk.

"You guys really need to stop arguing." I said to Jenna and Brokk as I gave each of them a long stare.

"If we just let Brokk go off on his own there is no telling what he might do. I can not have him going off to warn Lilith or the Guard about our plan." Jenna and Tuck nodded in agreement.

"I would never do that Callie!" Brokk yelled.

"You have already betrayed me once Brokk!"

"Callie, you know that I didn't have any choice. If I would have refused to turn you over to Lilith, I would be dead and she would have just sent someone else after you." He was starting to sound desperate.

"Okay, Brokk. I get it." I starting to feel really exasperated with him.

He was always so much sexier when I thought he was a bad boy. This puppy love coddling business was really starting to get on my nerves.

"I could take care of him for you, Callie." Tuck said with a grin as ran his fingers close to the edge of his sword.

I saw Brokk flinch and I had to hide my amusement.

"Okay guys. Really, that's enough."

I really did need to grip on these three before their fighting drove me insane.

"Brokk, you can stick with us. But if for one second I suspect that you are not on my side in this, I will let Tuck and his little friend take care of you." I said glancing back at the blade.

We all laughed. Well, except for Brokk of course.

20

I really did not have a plan. I knew that I needed to get to the palace, but that would not be easy. I had to make it into the city and past the guards to do it. This might have been easier to accomplish before they discovered Drake and started visiting it on a regular basis. Now they guarded the only doorway that I knew of into Petrona from where we were.

They have also been patrolling the part of the tunnel between the two cities. They have been working extra hard to cut the people of Drake off from the outside world. They have not even been able to get supplies or sell their crafts in weeks.

All the more reason for me to put a stop to Lilith. She was a tyrant. She did not care about anybody. She just wanted to toss her power around so that everyone would fear her.

Lilith made a huge mistake when she brought me here.

She thought that she could use me to her advantage. She thought that by displaying me to the citizens of Petrona like some kind of sideshow freak she would somehow boost her status another notch.

She murdered my parents to make sure that no one would come to my rescue. She tried to lock me away like some kind of animal. But she should know by now that she has very much underestimated me.

"We need to be ready for a fight as soon as we step back into the tunnel. There is no telling what Kailen has planned for us." Tuck said and then turned to Brokk.

"Brokk, are you going to be willing to fight the other guards if it comes down to that? Because it probably will."

"Yes, of course. I will do what I have to." Brokk answered.

"Good. We should leave out packs here and only take what we absolutely need. That should only be our weapons." Tuck gave us a fierce look.

"Tuck, you and I are the only ones with a weapon." I pointed out.

"I do not need a weapon!" Jenna explained. "I can fight with my hands and I will use fairy magic too if it comes to that. You should use it too, Callie. You are ready."

I nodded. I hoped that I was ready.

I hefted off my pack and arranged my sword so that I would have easier access to it when things got heated. I felt something hit my chest.

I looked down to see the gold coin hanging from its chain around my neck. Without even thinking, I grabbed it and gave a firm pull.

The necklace gave way and I threw the necklace and the coin that had been around my neck for more than ten years, into the tunnel.

I turned back to see Jenna staring cockeyed at me. "What was that all about?"

"I just didn't need it anymore." I said with an uneasy smile.

I looked over at Brokk to see that he was staring off into the direction that I had just thrown the necklace.

Then, he looked back at me and down to my naked finger. I suddenly became very aware of the weight of the heavy ring in my pocket.

I wanted to say something to reassure him that I still had it. I would never toss it away. It had belonged to his mother and I knew that it meant a lot to him.

"Is everybody ready?" Tuck asked pulling me from my thoughts.

I didn't know what I wanted to say to Brokk about the ring, so I didn't say anything at all. I just brushed past him into the tunnel.

"Let's get going." Jenna said as she followed me out.

We clung to the shadows once again as we approached the entrance to Drake. I did not know what to expect and I wanted to at least try to slip by unnoticed.

This time there was no music being played. It appeared that the party was over. I could still smell the faint woodsy aroma of the remaining campfires.

I felt Jenna come to a sudden stop at my side.

I looked up to find that my worst fears had come to life. Standing shoulder to shoulder across the tunnel was Kailen, his brother, and four other men. They were blocking our passage.

"What is this about Kailen?" I asked as I stepped from the shadows to the middle of the tunnel facing him.

"I warned you, Callie." He said. "We do not want any more trouble."

"Looks like you are starting trouble to me." Tuck moved to my side.

"It doesn't have to be this way for you, Tuck. You do not have to be a part of this. You are only going to get yourself killed." Kailen warned. "Leave her now and join with us. We will make sure that you are safe."

Tuck did not like that very much. He bowed up as if to charge Kailen, but Jenna placed a firm hand on his chest and he stopped in his tracks.

"I do not need a jerk like you to keep me safe!" He yelled. "And I have had to deal with a lot worse than taking down a few outcasts like you!"

"If that is the choice that you wish to make, so be it. But as long as you choose to fight alongside of Callie Rose, I will show no mercy." Kailen replied.

Callie Rose? This guy had turned into a real jerk.

"You know what you can do with your mercy!" Tuck was spitting bullets, he was so mad.

Kailen widened his stance and the other men followed suit. They had their hands on their hips, daring us to try to get passed them.

"What should we do Callie?" Jenna whispered.

With a slow but fierce tone, I answered. "Take them down."

The four of us fanned out forming a line of our own. We stood about ten feet in front of the outcasts. Someone only needed to take one step forward and the battle would be on.

To think, it was only about three weeks ago that I shared my first kiss with this man. Now I was about to send him to his grave. A cold shudder ran through me, but I shook it off. I could not let him stop me. Lilith's rein had to end, and it had to end today.

I reached up, my hand ready to pull my sword from its sheath. I glanced to my left to see that Jenna was at my elbow. She carried no weapon and I worried about her for just a moment. Tuck was just on the other side of her, his blade was already drawn. I knew that he would do whatever he had to do to protect Jenna.

I looked to my right and Brokk's piercing blue eyes met mine. He had no weapon either, but he was a Royal Guard himself. He knew how to handle himself in battle. He nodded that he was ready.

"Step aside Kailen." I called out. "This is the last time that I am going to ask."

"Callie, go back to the cavern. I have set you up a really nice place. You should be grateful. I could have just sent you on your way to roam these tunnels alone. Who knows what might have happened to you?"

"Nice try Kailen. But I am not going anywhere, except through this tunnel to Petrona. Now move!" This time I pulled out my sword as I yelled. The sound of the metal glinting off the sides of the sheath as it emerged shook me to my bones, in a good way. I was pumped and ready for the fight.

I stepped forward. My sword raised, ready to strike. I didn't even want to think about what I was about to do. The thought of what I had done to Sty and his friend was still fresh in my mind.

"Stand aside Kailen!" I said once more.

"I will NOT!" He yelled.

I charged onward. One of his men jumped forward to block my blow with a large shovel. I had no idea what was going on with Tuck, Jenna, or Brokk. My only focus was the large burly guy in front of me.

I pushed him backward and regained my stance. He came at me next. He had the shovel raised over his head and attempted to bring in it down hard.

I struck it with my blade and the end of the shovel went flying into the wall. I was almost proud of myself for a second. Until I realized that I had left him with a very sharp stake.

The wooden handle of the shovel had been sheared off at an odd angle, leaving him with a very effective spear.

He grinned and then jabbed the pole at my chest. I jumped back spreading my arms wide and curling my stomach in to avoid the blow. I had to struggle to regain my stance.

I was getting mad now. I slid my sword back into its sheath and went after him with my bare hands. He came at me with the wooden handle again. This time I grabbed the end of it and ripped it from his grip.

The look of surprise on his face was almost comical. I raised the handle as if I were a batter waiting for a pitch. Then I swung it with all of my might. It connected with the side of his head with a tremendous thump. He stood for a minute, unblinking. Then he collapsed to the floor.

I turned to see what was happening with the others.

Tuck was fighting with Kailen's brother and another guy. He was able to knock Kailen's brother down just long enough so that he could land a powerful fist to the dead center of the first guy's face.

Jenna had one of the smaller guys in a headlock and was pounding her fist into his face. He struggled to break free, but her size was to her advantage. She held onto him for dear life and never relented with her punches.

I looked for Brokk. I have to admit that I got a little worried when I didn't find him right away. It would be just like him to take off and leave us.

I heard a scuffle behind me and turn to see that Kailen had pulled Brokk a little further into the tunnel. Brokk was lying on the ground and Kailen was holding him up by his shirt collar. He had his fist pulled back and was about to strike.

I ran in their direction and started to raise the handle over my head. I was preparing to swing again, this time at Kailen. He must have saw me coming because he turned his head and looked up into my face just as I let loose and landed a hard blow across his back. He yelled out in pain and rolled off of Brokk onto his side on the floor.

I struggled to pull Brokk to his feet. He looked like he had taken a few good hits but he was okay. As soon as he was up, he turned back to Kailen. He drew back a leg and landed a hard kick to Kailen's ribcage. Then he kicked again and again. He would not stop.

"Brokk! Brokk!" I yelled at him repeatedly. After a few moments, he must have finally heard me. He pulled his focus from Kailen and looked at me.

"It's okay Brokk. That's enough." I said a little more gently.

I could see his face change as he began to pull himself from his blinding rage. Then all at once, he was standing in front of me with his arms wrapped around my shoulders tightly.

He was breathing heavily and he deepened his embrace until I could feel his breath at the back of my head. His hands wound in my hair.

"It's okay Brokk. I'm okay." I whispered to him. I felt his breathing begin to slow. Then suddenly he tensed again and pulled away from me.

Before I could blink, he was back on Kailen. He lifted him up and pounded his fist into Kailen's face.

"That is for kissing my future wife!" He yelled at Kailen and then hit him again.

Kailen was laid out on the floor, clutching his side. Blood trickled from his nose and mouth. He moaned in agony. I did not think that he would be causing any more trouble for a while.

We turned our focus back to Tuck and Jenna.

Tuck was still battling it out with Kailen's brother. I watched as I saw Tuck draw his sword. I held my breath, I was not sure that I wanted to see what would happen next. Tuck suddenly reversed the blade and using the thick metal handle, he struck his opponent across his temple. He staggered a little and then fell heavily to the floor.

We caught site of Jenna just as she jumped into the air and twisted with her leg straight out.

She looked like a ballerina, but she landed a devastating blow across the guy's chest. Once she was back on the ground, she landed a punch to the underside of his chin and sent him crashing backwards into the wall.

We all stood there in silence for a moment, struggling to catch our breath as we took in the carnage of our first fight.

Tuck wrapped one arm around Jenna's waist and silently they stepped over the fallen villagers and headed past Drake into the tunnel.

I watched them for a moment as they left. They were going to make a really great couple someday, when all of this was over. I pulled my eyes away and stared at the ground. I truly hoped that it would be over soon.

I looked up to find Brokk watching me. I didn't know whether I should be angry or amused. Maybe I was being too hard on him, but I still was not sure that I could fully trust him. Not to mention the fact that I had already had my full share of guy problems lately. I was not looking to go there again.

"Your future wife, huh?" I asked.

He just looked at me and shrugged.

21

Brokk and I had to hurry to catch up with Tuck and Jenna in the tunnel. We were all still a little bit exhausted from our fight with Kailen and the villagers.

"What should we do now?" Jenna asked.

"I think that we need to just lay low for a little while and recuperate." Brokk said. "It will still be a few more hours before the merchants close up for the night. Once most of the city has gotten home and gone to bed, it will be much easier to sneak in."

"He's right." Tuck agreed. "And if we do have to fight the Guard, it will be much easier if we are well rested."

It really had not been that long since we started out, but after the fight we had just been through I could definitely use a bite to eat and some water. Luckily, Jenna kept her pack on her since she didn't have a weapon strapped to her back. I was starting to think that a nap might not be so bad either.

We found a place that was tucked away, so hopefully we would not be disturbed. Jenna spread out her blanket so that we would not have to sit on the cold floor.

I munched on a beef stick and swigged some water, while Tuck and Jenna curled up with each other beside me.

Brock sat with his back propped against the wall. I offered him some water and he took it, smiling.

"Where did you learn to fight that way?" He asked quietly. Trying not to disturb the others.

"Jenna and Tuck taught me." I gestured toward them.

"You were pretty amazing back there. Thanks for getting that jerk off of me." He was smiling again.

"No problem. Thanks for defending my honor." I said with a giggle.

"It was the least that I could do." He bowed his head at me.

"Callie, I am truly sorry about everything that has happened. I know that you do not wish to hear it, but I really did try to save your parents. I wish that I could have gotten to them faster."

I stared at the floor to keep from meeting his eyes. I didn't know if that was something that I could ever forgive him for. I know that he is not the one that killed them. And I know that he went back to try to stop it. However, he knew what Lilith planned to do and he did not try to stop it soon enough.

He also came for me when she asked him. He knew then what she wanted me for. He may not have known that she was going to lock me away like her prisoner, but he knew that her intentions were not good.

"Callie?" He said softly.

This time I looked at him.

"I should never have let my anger and resentment get the better of me. It was not until we were traveling through the tunnel to Petrona that I realized how much I care for you."

"Well, thanks I guess. I really don't know what else to say to you Brokk."

"You don't have to say anything. I just wanted you to know." It was him that looked away this time.

"Brokk, let's just get through the next few days. Then we can talk. Right now I think that we really need to focus on what we are about to do."

"Okay." He smiled. Then he pulled me to him. I laid my head on his chest as he continued to lean his back against the wall. I could hear the beating of his heart and feel the gentle rise and fall of his chest as he breathed. It was enough to lull anybody to sleep. Anybody but me, that is. I was to amped up to sleep.

In just a few short hours, we would be entering the city. I had no idea how everything was going to go down, but the one thing that I knew for sure was there was definitely going to be fight. A bad one.

Apparently, none of us could rest for very long. Our nerves had gotten the better of us, I guess. Jenna and Tuck started to stir, so Brokk and I got up too.

Once we found that we could not put it off any longer, we gathered ourselves together and prepared to enter the city. Most of the merchants and citizens would have already gone home and hopefully were asleep in their beds.

Brokk volunteered to go in first. He has been one of the Guard for years and was friends with many of them. If anyone were near, hopefully they would not think anything of him being there.

We waited just inside the doorway for him to return and give us the okay. I could not just stand still and wait, so I found myself pacing nervously.

"Calm down, Callie." Jenna was mothering me as per her usual.

"I can't. He has been gone too long. Something must have happened." I said anxiously.

"He is probably just trying to find out where all the sentries are posted. He will be back soon." Tuck said.

That really did not make me feel any better. Although Brokk was able to track me down on the surface and bring me back with no problem, I still did not think that he was much of a fighter. Kailen was able to overpower him far too easily for my liking.

A few minutes later, we heard some noise on the other side of the door. I rushed to open it but Tuck pulled me back.

"Shhh, just wait." He whispered.

I stood completely still with my back against Tuck. He kept one hand on my shoulder, holding me in place.

My heart was beating in a frenzy, I was so scared. I don't know if it was the weird bond that I shared with Brokk or if it was something else, but I felt this strange desire to want to protect him.

I had no idea why I felt as if he could not take care of himself. He had managed to find me and bring me here, and no matter how hard I struggled and fought, he never even flinched. He was a trained guard and should be able to handle nearly anything, but I just could not stop myself from worrying.

There was a loud click and the door slowly started to open. I held my breath. A tall figure slid through the doorway and shut it back. He slowly began walking towards us, but something was not right. There was sort of a hitch to his walk that made him sway to one side as he moved. I wanted to run to him but Tuck only held me tighter,

"Callie…" I heard him say with difficulty. I broke free from Tuck's gasp and ran to him.

It was definitely Brokk, and he had been hurt. Aside from his obvious limp, his clothes were dirty and disheveled.

His face was swollen and scraped along his forehead and across his cheek.

"What happened?" I asked frantically as I pulled his arm around my shoulder and attempted to help support him as he walked. Tuck and Jenna helped me sit him down with his back propped against the wall. My hands flew about his face in an attempt to determine his injuries, but I was too afraid to actually touch him.

He reached up, grabbed one of my hands, pulled it to his heart, and held it there as his head fell forward.

"Brokk what's wrong? Tell me what happened." I pleaded. I was on the verge of tears.

"You do love me." He said quietly. A small smile spread across his face.

"I am worried about you Brokk." I shook my head back and forth, trying to clear my mind. Why would he say that? I was frightened and worried about him, but that didn't mean that I loved him.

Jenna offered him some water and he drank heartily. After a while, he seemed to be recovering a bit. He began to tell us of how he entered the city, and hid as he canvassed the streets, making sure that the citizens were in there homes and safe. He came across an occasional guard on patrol and managed to remain unseen.

He made his way all the way up to the palace. There were guards at various locations surrounding it.

He attempted to make his way to the back through the garden. It was there that he was caught off guard.

He had just climbed over the tall rock wall that surrounded the rear of the palace and the garden. He attempted to make his way to one of the rear doors close to the kitchen. The servants used this entrance throughout the day but he had hoped that they all would have gone home for the night.

Just as he made his way up onto the large marble patio, he felt a large hand grab hold of him and spin him around. He only got a brief look at the guard because in an instant he got a fist to his face and was stumbling backwards. He did not immediately recognize the guard and was sure that he should know everyone who worked within a close proximately to the palace.

The guard hit him a few more times and then held him with his hands behind his back.

He brought Brokk into the stony basement under the palace and threw him into a cell. As Brokk tried to fight, another guard joined the first and they began kicking and beating him. After they finally left him, it was Bree who came to his rescue.

She had heard the guards talking about the man that they had just locked up and she could tell by their description that it must have been Brokk. She snuck away and stole the keys from a large hook near the basement door. She turned Brokk free and he eventually managed to make it his way back here.

"The queen must have brought in more men from another Fae colony." Tuck said.

This was not good news. Our odds were already pretty bad, but now we had no idea what we faced. There could be hundreds more, and none of the new guards would know Brokk or remember my family.

I slumped to the floor in front of Brokk. He never released my hand. He just held his arm out toward me as I extended mine toward him. I gave his hand a gentle squeeze, but I did not look at him. Instead, I rested the side of my face on my bent knees.

"Maybe this was a mistake." I said in a low voice. "Maybe we would be better off if we had just stayed back in the cavern. There is no way that we can overcome an Army of men that large."

"Don't give up, Callie." Jenna said softly in her sweet little pixie voice. "There has to be a way. This is what you were born for. Your mother was the queen, Lilith is only a stand in. Now that Queen Faylinn is gone, you are the true queen. You cannot just spend the rest of your days hiding out in some cavern. The people of this city need you."

"What can I do, Jenna? There are only four of us. We can't even ask the people of Drake for help. They were willing to fight us just to keep us from getting to the city. They don't want any part of something that might just cause another war for them."

"Why not use your fairy magic?" Tuck asked. "I have never seen anyone as powerful as the two of you." He gestured toward Jenna then looked back at me.

"The queen has fairy magic too." I started to say.

"Not like yours." I looked up to see Brokk looking intently at me. "You are a direct descendant of the royal blood line. No one else should have magic as strong as yours."

I looked at Jenna, studying her hard. "Jenna does." I stated.

She looked surprised. "No, not like yours Callie."

"I have watched you train, Jenna. Your magic is every bit as strong as mine."

"How can that be?" Brokk asked as he eyed Jenna.

"I don't know what you are talking about." She said defensively.

"Jenna, you do have an affinity for all of the elements." Tuck said gently. "It is a very rare occurrence, but it is something that you should be proud of."

"I'm sorry." Jenna was shaking her head. "I just don't understand how that could be. I mean, I know that I can use all of the elements, but I am nowhere near as powerful as Callie. You have seen her. You know how strong she is."

"I also know how strong you are." Tuck smiled as he wrapped an arm around her shoulder and pulled her to him.

Everyone was quiet for a while. I was willing to bet that we were all thinking about the same thing. If I was this powerful because of my bloodline, where did Jenna's power come from?

That was a mystery that would have to be solved at another time, right now, we needed to prepare for a fight.

"Jenna, do you think that between the two of us we can do this?" I asked her.

"Yes, I think that we can handle it. We will need to stay together, we would be more lethal that way."

"What will we be doing?" Brokk asked, as he peered up to me with his gorgeous sapphire eyes. "We can not just sit here and do nothing."

"We will fight until we have to use magic." I said. "But I don't think you are up to it Brokk. You still need to recuperate from your last run in with the Guard."

"I am fine." He said as he struggled to his feet. He winced a little but quickly straightened himself to prove that he was okay. "I will not let you go in there without me."

"He's right." Tuck said. "We need all of the help we can get, even with the magic."

I looked at Brokk. He was still a little bruised but he was pulling himself together pretty quickly.

That still did nothing to stop my heart from skipping a beat each time that I saw him try to hide his pain. What other choice did I have? We did need him.

"Okay." I said. "But we will all stick together. I don't want any of you getting hurt because of me."

"These people deserve a fair and kind ruler. This is for all of them. We can do this." Jenna said. Her words revealing the excitement that was starting to build for the battle.

I nodded. "Let's go."

22

We stood just outside of the tunnel door to ready ourselves. This time we opened our wings. We may need them if we wanted to win this fight. I wanted to use them to fly to the palace but Tuck thought that it would draw too much attention to soon.

This was the first time that I got to see Brokk's wings. During the rest of the times that I had spent with him, I was still under my parents glamour spell.

I was in complete awe. His wings were large and shimmering silver. They were outlined in a deep gold and they were covered in gold scrollwork similar to mine.

I couldn't help but wonder what that could mean, but I did understand why my mother would agree that we should marry. It was almost as if he were made for me.

As much as I hated to, I had to push those thoughts from my mind. I had a battle to get ready for.

I pulled my sword around so that it was hanging at my side. I could easily reach across my body and pull it out if I needed to.

I followed Tuck and Jenna into the deserted streets and Brokk was not far behind me. He was still limping and he was apparently having trouble keeping up. I slowed my pace a little so that he would still be able to see me, but I still kept a close eye on Jenna and Tuck.

I watched as the pair ducked back into the shadows. Jenna had turned and jerked her head, signaling me to take cover. Brokk must have saw it too because he grabbed my hand and pulled me in to a dark alleyway. He placed himself between me and the street blocking me from the guard that strolled whistling by.

Thankfully, he did not even look our way as he passed, but we waited a few more minutes just in case.

Brokk held me to him with one arm around my back as he watched over his shoulder for the guard. I took in a deep breath and closed my eyes as his honeysuckle and wood scent left me heady. I opened my eyes to find Brokk staring down at me with a sly smile on his face. I gave him a stern look, but that only made him smile wider.

"Callie." He whispered softly against my ear. "Before we go any farther there is something that I need to do."

I looked at him inquisitively for a moment as his eyes held mine. He tilted his head slightly and I felt like my heart would leap right out of my chest.

He reached up and took the back of my head into his hand as he gently pulled me forward. He firmly pressed his lips to mine.

I resisted and tried to pull away but he held me in place. I opened my eyes to find that I was staring straight into his. I froze as I felt a flood of emotion start to fill me and tears started to swirl against my eyelashes. I found it impossible t resist him any longer, so I reached up and locked both of my arms around his neck and kissed him back.

It started out soft and sweet but soon a desperate passion ignited between us both. I opened my mouth slightly and allowed him to explore further with his tongue as I did the same in turn.

The kiss grew deeper by the second and I struggled to breath, but I did not want to let him go. He lowered his arms to my hips and I responded by pulling myself up and wrapping my legs around his waist. I felt as if I could not get close enough to him. Right then at that moment I never wanted to be anywhere else in the world.

"Uh, hey." I heard a soft voice say.

I pulled back from Brokk and peered over the top of his shoulder to see Tuck and Jenna staring at us from the end of the alley. Suddenly I remembered where I was and why I was here. I felt an instant heat flood my face and I was sure that I must have turned ten shades of red.

I looked back to Brokk who was smiling once again. He placed one more soft kiss on my lips then I untangled my legs from him and he lowered me back down on my feet.

"We'll be right there." Brokk called. "Just give us a second."

"Okay, well hurry up." Jenna said. She and Tuck slipped back into the shadow on the street.

Brokk looked back at me. "Callie, I am sorry but I thought that this may have been my last chance to set things right. I did not want to leave this earth without ever even have kissed you. I just wish that I had done it sooner. Maybe you wouldn't have kissed that Kailen guy if I had."

I rolled my eyes. He was trying to be sweet, but the guy in him was shining through. "Brokk, I am sorry about Kailen. I wish that I never would have even met him. But I can promise you one thing, he never kissed me like that."

He smiled and his chest swelled with pride. I had to roll my eyes again. Typical guy. He grabbed my hands and placed one more kiss on the top of my forehead. Then he reached over and to my surprise, he stuck his hand into the pocket of my blue jeans and pulled out the ring.

"How did you know that was there?"

"I couldn't miss that lump against your leg."

His smile widened and he slid the ring back onto my finger.

"I know that we can't talk about everything that happened right now, but I do love you Callie. Will you please wear my ring?"

Tears once again. I just couldn't help myself. I swear I did nothing but cry anymore.

"Of course I'll wear your ring."

He kissed me again. Slow and deep as he picked me up by my waist.

"Are you ready?" He asked hesitantly.

"Let's go kick some butt."

We rounded the corner onto the street and found Tuck and Jenna waiting for us in the next alley. The two guys led the way this time and Jenna followed along beside me.

"What was that all about?" She asked leaning in to me.

"I don't know. Something just came over me. I could not stop myself." I said with a giggle.

"Will you ever learn?" She laughed and so did I as I shook my head no.

I looked up to find that we were getting close to the palace. This is where things were going to start getting tricky. The guards would be more concentrated in this area in order to protect the queen.

I stared up at the tall white turrets, my palms we starting to sweat. I rubbed my hands together in an effort to help me concentrate on what I needed to do.

If we tried to take out the Guard right now, they would alert the queen and her personal guards and she would probably flee. But if I tried to go straight for the queen there would be too many guards coming to her rescue that we would have to fight. There was no easy way to do this.

"Let's just try to get as far as we can before we start trying to take anybody down." I said.

"Okay, nobody do anything until they absolutely have to. The closer we are to the queen, the better." Jenna instructed.

Everyone agreed and we pushed forward. We made it all the way up the front marble stairs when suddenly the large wooden door flew open and Bree stepped out.

She looked to me and then at Brokk as if trying to ascertain what was going on. "What are you doing here?" She asked, bewildered.

"Bree," Brokk said. "I want you to go straight to your room and lock the door. Do not come out until I come for you."

"What are you talking about Brokk? I just helped you escape. This is about her isn't it?" She nodded toward me, sounding angry.

"Bree, you just need to do as I ask." He insisted.

"Why? Why do you have to keep doing things to anger the queen. You just keep getting yourself hurt Brokk!" She was starting to sound desperate.

Tuck and Jenna looked at each other and then turned to look back at me. I was not sure what to say or do. Bree had always been the one to help me when I was locked away here, but I never got the impression that she really liked me. I always felt like it was a chore for her. Now I was beginning to wander what her relationship was to Brokk.

"Brokk, if she is not going to listen to you, then we need to lock her up ourselves." Tuck motioned toward Bree.

Brokk spun to face Tuck. His anger showed on his face. His nostrils flared, his body grew rigid. I moved to place myself between the two of them, holding my hands up to Brokk.

"You will not touch her!" He growled.

"Brokk!" I said desperately. "Nobody wants Bree to get hurt. It would only be to protect her."

His eyes met mine and I could see him begin to calm instantly.

"I won't let anything happen to her. I promise." I said to him more quietly.

He nodded and turned to face Bree. "Please Bree, let's go up to your room."

She looked at each of us and then nodded to Brokk. He took her by the elbow and led her inside. They walked to the top of the stairs and into what used to be my old room. I waited at the bottom of the stairs with the others.

I heard a door close and then a click as the lock was turned. Brokk appeared at the top of the stairs looking forlorn. I met him halfway as he descended the stairs. I took his hand and looked deeply into his eyes for a moment. I still couldn't figure out why he got so angry.

"She's going to be okay, Brokk." I whispered.

He nodded in acknowledgement. We moved through the palace toward the queen's sleeping quarters. I found myself a little surprised that we had not run into any of the guards by then.

"Something is not right." I whispered to Brokk.

"I sense it too. The palace was surrounded by guards when I tried to get in earlier."

We made it to the door of the queen's chamber. I pressed my ear to the door but I was not able to hear any sound coming from inside. I gently tried to turn the knob but it was locked.

"I'll kick it in." Whispered Tuck. He drew back and with one hard thump of his shoulder the door flew open.

We rushed inside with Jenna and me in the lead. Tuck and Brokk stood on either side of the door. Brokk reached up and flipped on the lights.

It took a few seconds for my eyes to adjust to the brightness after spending so long in the darkness of the tunnels. I rubbed my eyes hard and looked up to find that we were surrounded by at least thirty of the queen's guards and she was nowhere in sight.

"It was a trap!" Jenna exclaimed. "Somebody must have warned them that we were coming!"

"It must have been the Drakes! Damn!" Tuck said. He drew his sword as the guards closed in on us.

"What do we do Callie?" Jenna asked as two of the guards rushed towards her.

I started to panic, everything was happening so quickly that I barely had time to think. I held up my hands and called to Erion, the spirit of the air. He was there in an instant. I threw my hands forward and a strong gust of wind was sent into the approaching soldiers. They flew backward and crashed into the wall with a hard thud.

That took at least a third of them down, but the rest pulled out their weapons. They looked ready to fight. There was still too many, I had to try again. This time as I looked to Erion, I spun my arm around in a circular motion. A few seconds later a small funnel of wind appeared before me. I threw my arm out toward the guards, and the funnel followed suit. It flew into the soldiers and ripped the swords from their hands. I could see the silvery glint of the weapons spinning around inside of the tube of air.

"Be careful with that Callie!" I heard Jenna call to me over the sound of the rushing wind.

I lowered my hand gently and the twirling wind started to slow. The swords were softly placed onto the ground.

I saw Brokk bend down and pick one up out of the corner of my eye. The rest of the guardsman held their hands up in surrender.

"Where is Lilith?" I asked the guard standing out in front of the others. He must have been some sort of commander because he had lots of stars and stripes sewn onto his uniform.

He looked around hesitantly, but he did not speak.

I motioned for Brokk to move toward him. Brokk was there in an instant. He wrapped an arm around the guy's neck and held a blade to his throat.

I asked again. "Where is Lilith?"

"Sh-she's gone." He stuttered. "She took some of the guards and left."

"Where?" I asked again. "Where has she gone?"

When he did not answer, Brokk tightened his grip on the guy's neck. "Answer her!" He yelled.

"I-I think they went to the surface." He choked out.

"When?" I demanded. "How long have they been gone?"

"O-only about," He paused gasping for air. "Thirty minutes."

"We can still catch her." Brokk said.

"No." I said, looking at each of them. "You stay here and keep an eye on the guards. I can do this on my own."

"Callie, wait." Jenna yelled. "You are going to get yourself killed. We should all go."

"If we all go the guard will have time to reorganize. I need you more here." I turned and looked at the commander.

"Do you know who I am?"

He peered up at me, but he did not answer.

"I am Calliope Rose, daughter of the former Queen Faylinn and King Elvin. Do you know what that means? It means that I am your true queen. You will serve me or you will die." I glared at him. I was being so serious that I almost wanted to laugh at myself, but I held my composure. "From now on you will answer to Brokk or to me. Is that understood?"

"B-but, Brokk is just a foot soldier." He started to say.

"You will address me as your queen!" I yelled. "And Brokk is my betrothed, which makes him your future king! I suggest you start acting like it!"

Brokk jerked his head up to look at me, as did Jenna and Tuck. I really did not have time to explain myself, and I really did not know what I would say. It just sort of came out in the heat of the moment.

I turned and ran for the door.

23

As soon as I was outside, I opened my wings and leaped into air. I soared over the city looking down at the twinkling lights that lit the streets. The wind washed over me, it was so exhilarating that I could not help but giggle. I looked around and spotted a few guards posted around the perimeter but they never bothered to look up to notice me.

I brought myself down at the opening to the tunnel that led to the surface. I remembered that it had taking Brokk hours to bring me through it when I first came to Petrona, so the queen could not have gotten far.

I started running through the tunnel as fast as I could but I feared that I would not have the endurance to keep up such a pace for very long. I tried to extend my wings, they were able to open fully but there was not a lot of room for error. If I was not careful, I would damage them on the sharp rocky walls. I tried pushing them straight out and that helped a little.

I carefully picked myself up and flew. I bobbed around a little at first and that made me a bit nervous, but soon I had gotten the hang of it. I pointed my body like an arrow. I felt like superman as I held out my arms, willing myself to go faster.

The slick inky floor of the tunnel soared past me in a blur. The smell of the damp stale air filled my nose. My sinuses burned from it, but I pressed on.

I slowed myself after traveling for at least twenty minutes. Surely, I was getting close by now. I listened carefully for the sounds of footsteps or whispers. I thought that I heard the sound of something moving up ahead, so I landed onto my feet. I walked at a quick pace, trying as hard as possible not too make to much noise and draw attention to myself just yet.

I peered ahead and could just make out the silhouettes of the guard. I froze and moved against the wall. I took a moment to pull myself together. Now that I had found them, what was I going to do?

I stepped out from the wall and closed my eyes. I called to Demi, the earth spirit and soon felt the ground under my feet begin to rumble.

I heard screaming from up ahead as a large mound of earth and rock rose up from the floor, blocking their escape.

I stood in the center of the tunnel as Lilith and her guardsman began to run back towards me. They stopped when they finally noticed me standing there.

"You insolent child!" Lilith screamed as she moved to close the gap between us. "How dare you show your face here! I should have finished you when I had the chance!"

"That is quite enough." I said in the most stern voice that I could muster. "Your time here is over. You may have been able to manipulate my parents into giving up their kingdom, but I am not as easily fooled."

She stared at me for a moment and then let out a loud booming laugh that echoed throughout the tunnel. "Guards! Get her!" She called.

Several of the guards rushed toward me. I help my palm out to them and called Erion to push them back. They were frozen in their tracks as they fought against the wind to carry themselves forward.

"Give it up Lilith!" I yelled. "You are no queen! Nor have you ever been! You are barely even Fae. You have even lost your fairy magic. You are pathetic and your tyranny ends today!"

She moved toward me and I pulled out my sword. Her eyes grew large in surprise. "Faylinn's sword! Where did you get that?" She cried.

I took my stance, holding the sword up and ready to strike. She reached her arm out and one of the guards handed her a sword of her own. I stepped out before she had time to strike and swung, but she was fast. She deflected my blow with ease. I came right back at her with another.

I spun around hard and swung my sword out in front of me. She was able to block my sword with hers but my force sent her stumbling backwards.

It only took a moment for her to regain her balance and she came at me again with a vengeance.

We fought until I felt like I would not be able to raise the sword again. My arms burned from fatigue and I was panting for breath. Each swing of my blade was met blow for blow. I had to end this.

I raised my sword, swung with all of my might, and came down hard across her blade slicing it in half. The sound of metal clanking across the floor echoed all around us. I looked up to see a large pool of blood spreading across her chest.

Lilith looked down at her cut, and raised her hand to cover her chest. Her eyes were frantic and she yelled for one of her guards. I asked Erion to release the wind and allowed them to come to her. The others just stood their ground watching the scene.

I called to Demi and opened the exit to the surface.

"Take her now and do not return." I said to the guard kneeling at Lilith's side. He lifted her up and carried her into the darkness. I watched them until they were completely out of site.

I turned to the remaining soldiers. "If you choose to continue to follow Lilith then you may go, but if you wish to serve me you are welcome to stay."

They all stared at me for a few seconds and slowly, one by one they stepped in the direction of Petrona.

I called to the sprits one last time and closed the exit once again with large boulders. If Lilith survived, I did not want her to return.

I followed the soldiers back to Petrona.

I stepped into a city that was just beginning to stir with life. The merchants were preparing to open their shops, and I could smell the scent of delicious bacon and biscuits cooking.

The citizens stopped to stare as I was escorted to the palace. I nodded my head at each of them as I passed.

In the palace, I found Jenna and Tuck lounging on the sofas in the living area.

"What is this all about?" I asked in shock.

"Brokk has everything under control." Tuck answered, nodding toward the back of the house.

"I hope so." I said as I rushed to find him.

Brokk was standing outside in the garden behind the huge glass windows of the dining room. He had the guardsman all line up in neat little rows and he paced back and forth in front of them. I watched as the guards who escorted me back joined the ranks. One of them spoke and then Brokk turned to look at me.

Comprehension showed briefly on his face as he realized that I was back and what that could have meant.

I instantly ran for the door and before I knew it, he was inside the hall and wrapping his arms around me. He lifted me up by my waist and slowly spun me around.

"Callie, you are okay."

"I am." I said quietly and he bent his head forward and kissed me deeply. My reactions to his kisses began to get more and more intense. When his lips met mine, I felt my entire body shudder from my head down to my toes. I deepened the kiss and pulled him closer.

I am not sure who pulled away first, but we both stood staring breathless into each other's eyes.

"Is it over?" He asked.

"I doubt that it will ever be over, but she is gone."

"You didn't kill her?" He asked in astonishment.

"No, I only wounded her. Then I banished her to the surface and sealed the tunnel. Hopefully, that will be enough."

"I hope so too."

That evening we held a small celebration in the palace. We ate heartily and laughed until our sides ached. The housekeepers prepared a room for each of us to sleep, I refused to sleep in the queen's chambers until it had been completely stripped of any trace of Lilith. That goes for the rest of the house as well. No more stark, white everything.

Bree volunteered to take on the task of redecorating. After Brokk had gotten things under control, he had released her from my room. It turned out that she was his little sister and that the queen demoted her to servant after my parents left. No wonder she was so bitter.

The commander of the Guard called the citizens together and introduced me as their new queen. Most seemed to cheer, but not all. I would have to prove myself in the future to them. In addition, I would have to be careful with who to trust.

The next day was filled with the task of creating a council and reorganizing the political side of the monarchy. I insisted that elections be held so that the people could appoint those that they trusted to the various positions.

Brokk stayed on in the palace but he chose a room on a different wing than mine to give me some space. We ate every meal together and spent most evenings in each other's company either reading or walking in the garden.

It's funny that my parents had chosen him for me when I was just a baby, but somehow it felt as if he was made for me and I was made for him. I easily forgave him for the past few weeks, admitting that I had over reacted. In addition, I began to trust him again.

He took over as the head of the guard and handled himself quite well. He would make a great King someday.

Tuck and Jenna stayed on as my assistants. They found a small house in the city and were quite content.

I had not heard anymore from Lilith, but I knew that it was only a matter of time until she resurfaced. There is no way that she would give up that easily.

###

Connect with Me Online:

Webpage
http://ccjacksonbooks.com

Twitter
http://twitter.com/ccjacksonbooks

My Blog
http://ccjacksonbooks.blogspot.com

Facebook
http://facebook.com/ccjacksonbooks

Facebook Fan Page
http://facebook.com/ccjacksonfanpage